Star Bores
The Novel

Star Bores
The Novel

Steve Barlow
and
Steve Skidmore

Illustrated by Paddy Mounter

SHAFTESBURY, DORSET · BOSTON, MASSACHUSETTS · MELBOURNE, VICTORIA

First published in Great Britain in 1999 by
Element Children's Books
Shaftesbury, Dorset SP7 8BP

Published in the USA in 1999 by
Element Books, Inc.
160 North Washington Street,
Boston MA 02114

Published in Australia in 1999 by
Element Books and distributed by
Penguin Australia Limited,
487 Maroondah Highway, Ringwood,
Victoria 3134

Cover illustration by Chris Smedley.
Cover design by Alison Withey Design.
Typeset by DTG Design, Dorchester.
Printed and bound in Great Britain by Biddles Ltd, Guildford and King's Lynn

British Library Cataloguing in Publication data available.
Library of Congress Cataloging in Publication data available.

ISBN 1 902618 76 9

Contents

Star Bores
The Novel

A story of unbelievable heroism, unspeakable villainy, and unlimited merchandising opportunities . . .

Digitally Remastered in PAGEOVISION with SURROUNDWORDS™

May the Farce be with you!

Long, long, ago in a galaxy far, far, far, far, away . . .

Well, when we say long ago, we mean a fairly long time ago, not all THAT long ago – for instance, not right at the beginning of the Universe because everything was very hot then, and the highest form of life was a sort of worm that wasn't much more intelligent than the average daytime TV host – but much longer ago than when you could wear polyester pants without being laughed at, or your last birthday. And when we say far away, we don't mean all the way at the other end of the Universe – obviously, we wouldn't know anything about it because of worm holes – but a lot farther than, say, the next rest stop on the freeway . . .

Episode IV – A New Hype . . .

Wait a minute – what do you mean, Episode IV?

What do you mean, what do I mean?

I mean what happened to Episodes I, II, and III?

Ah, well, you see, there are IX Episodes altogether . . .

Did you say IX?!

Yes – but we've got to start somewhere and I reckon Episode IV is a real humdinger . . .

But why not start at Episode I?

Aha!

What?

Aha!

Could you be a bit more specific? If we start in the middle, where do we go from there?

Well, I thought we could do the beginning next . . .

The beginning? As a sequel to the middle?

Well, it couldn't be a sequel, could it, because it happens before. We'd have to call it a prequel.

I call it ridiculous! Why can't we just start at the beginning?

Why indeed!

Oh well, let's just keep going, OK? Roll the credits . . . cue music . . .

What do you mean, cue music? This is a book, we don't have any music.

Well, I'm sure the readers will want some music.

What do they expect for a few measly bucks, the Boston Symphony Orchestra? Oh, well, if you insist: all together now . . .

"Dah – *Dah*
Dadadad *Deeeeee* Dah
Dadadad *Deeeeee* Dah
Da da da *Daaaaaah* . . ."

The Empire is in turmoil. The Rebel forces of the
Grand Order Of Democratic, Independent,
Emancipated Societies (GOODIES) are at war
with the Empire's dreaded enforcement agency,
the Bureau for the Advancement of Destruction,
Depravity and Incredibly Evil Schemes (BADDIES).
GOODIES spies have managed to steal the plans
for the BADDIES' new secret weapon, an armored
space station with the firepower to vaporize
entire planets, known as the Moon of Doom™.
Fleeing from the dreaded BADDIES, Princess Liar
Origami of the planet Alcapone knows that only
she and the stolen plans she carries can bring
hope to the hard-pressed Rebels . . .

CHAPTER ONE
Gotcha!

Patrolbeing Fibaci of the Galactic Police lounged in the saddle of his gleaming spacecycle as it hovered in a parking orbit behind a small asteroid.

He was bored. Sector Omega was a dead-end assignment, far removed from the spaceways. Nothing ever happened out here.

Fibaci was a Kojakian. Most of the officers in the Galactic Traffic Patrol were. Kojakians were the best cops in the galaxy because they each had a flashing blue light on top of their heads. They didn't have a *hat* with a flashing blue light on top of their heads – they just had a flashing blue light on top of their heads. They were also dedicated, unimaginative, and easily bribed.

In short, they were perfect for the job.

Just as Fibaci was wondering whether to pursue his inquiries into the latest gangland slaying on the lawless planet of Toonilooni, or to scoot down to Al's Cosmic Diner for a taco, a spaceship hurtled past doing at least Warp Eight. Fibaci glanced at the Speed Limit sign hovering just beyond his asteroid. It clearly said, "Warp 4."

Fibaci grinned to himself and lowered his visor.

All *righty* !

He twisted the handgrip to gun the bike's powerful twin Ruggrat and Diaper PP3 engines, and rocketed out of his hiding place at Warp Nine.

Fibaci grinned to himself as he bent low over the handlebars, the engines howling beneath him. From its markings, Fibaci identified the speeding vessel as a Senator's ship. A speeding ticket for a Senator's ship would lead to a big arrest – or a big bribe. Either way was fine with Fibaci. His blue light rotated faster with excitement.

He switched his ultrasiren on.

WOooWOooWOooWOooWOooWOoo . . .

Seconds later, a high-powered customized Halley-Davidson spacebike rocketed past Fibaci as if he were standing still. It was followed by several huge wedge-shaped somethings. The wash from their mighty engines sent Fibaci's tiny one-man spacecycle tumbling out of control. Desperately fighting his bucking machine, Fibaci plowed into an asteroid that seemed to consist entirely of mud . . . at least, Fibaci *hoped* it was mud.

With a quivering tentacle, Patrolbeing Fibaci wiped glop from his eyes and stared after the rapidly disappearing ships.

"What in the galaxy was *that*?" he gasped.

"That" was the fleet of Star Crushers commanded by Dark Visor.

The Dread Lord leaned back in the leather saddle of his Megahog chopper, arms raised to the handlebars. Before him stretched the gleaming forks. Behind him swept the highly chromed exhaust, rumbling with barely contained power.

Dark Visor's cloak streamed behind him. He wore a tight-fitting suit of black plasti-leather, decorated with studs and chains. This mean-looking outfit gave protection against the deadly vacuum of space, laser fire, and even small meteorites.

The Dread Lord changed down a gear with a booted foot, twisted the throttle with a gloved hand, and dove at the Senator's ship, guns blazing.

From the bridge of the leading Star Crusher, Admiral Pitta watched Dark Visor's relentless attack on the defenseless vessel.

"That is one mean dude," he murmured.

Captain Needit nodded. "No lie!"

The Admiral flicked a switch. His amplified voice boomed through the corridors of the Star Crusher.

"Prepare to board the Senator's ship."

Swarms of armored Stomptroopers hurried to obey.

Aboard the Senator's ship, all was chaos. Princess Liar Origami staggered as the stricken vessel swayed and juddered under the withering hail of fire.

Captain Antifreeze strode onto the bridge.

"Abandon ship!" he ordered. "Women and children first!"

Liar whirled to face the panic-stricken commander. "Captain, will you please take off that dress, put down that teddy bear, and *listen* to me?"

"The deflector shields are down," moaned the Captain.

"No, they're not," said the Princess confidently.

"Yes they *are*," insisted Captain Antifreeze. "We'll be boarded any minute!"

"No, we won't. Chill out, Antifreeze. We'll be landing on Alcapone soon."

The Captain bit his nails. "This ship isn't going to make it to Alcapone. The plans you're carrying will never reach the Rebels. We're all doomed. Doomed!" He raced from the bridge, shouting, "Make way for Teddy! Bear coming through!"

Alone on the deserted bridge, Princess Liar stood in thought for a moment. Then she beckoned to a small droid, waiting in the shadows.

"Doo-weep?"

Dark Visor strode through the corridors of the captured ship, his boot heels striking sparks from the deck. His rasping breath echoed from the walls. He halted as two Stomptroopers appeared, dragging a struggling figure.

Princess Liar glared up at the Dread Lord.

"Dark Visor!" she snapped. "You'vc got some nerve, coming here."

Visor stared down at her. "Well, well. If it isn't Minnie Mouse."

"Leave my hairstyle out of this!" Liar stamped her foot.

Two more troopers approached, marching two droids at gunpoint. One looked like a moving garbage can; the other was a humanoid shape. It slouched along in a surly fashion, muttering sourly to itself.

"We found these two hiding in the cargo bay, sir," reported the leading trooper.

The Dread Lord turned to the humanoid droid. "I see you're a diplomatic droid."

"Yes indeed, sir. Politeness is my middle name." The humanoid robot's metallic features suddenly twisted into a sneer. "Mind you, my first name is 'Drop' and my last name is 'Dead,' copper." The droid spat a drop of oil onto one of Visor's polished boots.

Visor pointed a finger at the droid. An arc of electric fire leaped from his hand, and the ill-mannered machine gave a screech of electronic agony.

"Oh, I am sorry sir. I seem to have a malfunction in my politeness chip . . . you big palooka! Oops! I do apologize again," whined the droid. "I'm Doe Raymefar, and this bucket of bolts here," he paused to give the smaller droid a vicious kick, "is Sola Teedoe."

The small droid snarled, "Drathatfrattlerat." Then it snickered. "*Hih hih hih hih* . . . beep."

Visor gave an irritated gesture. "Dispose of them."

Princess Liar began to struggle again. "Leave them alone!" she yelled.

Visor gave her a considering look. "So, these droids are of value to you? Then you can save them by telling me where you have hidden the plans."

"I don't know what you're talking about."

The Dread Lord took the Princess's chin in one gloved hand. "I think you do. I mean the plans for the Empire's new secret weapon, the ones that were stolen by GOODIES spies and passed on to you."

"You'll never pin that rap on me, Visor."

"We shall see. So, what shall I do with your droids?"

"Leave them out of this."

"I think I'll have them melted down for scrap."

The Princess began to wail. "Sure, melt them down. Just don't send them to that planet out there."

Dark Visor glanced out of the port at the orange-yellow planet spinning beneath the ship. The desert world of Toonilooni, home of the worst scum in the Galaxy.

Visor turned his evil gaze back to the Princess. "Or I could have them torn to bits before your very eyes."

The Princess sobbed in terror. "Anything, anything,

just as long as you don't send them to that planet out there."

"How's about I reprogram their memory banks with an ice pick?"

"Yes!" howled the Princess. "Whatever! Melt them! Tear them apart! Do your worst. Just don't send them to that planet out there!"

"Hurrr, hurrr, hurrr." The Dread Lord gave an evil chuckle. "I know what I'm going to do. I'm going to send these droids to that planet out there!"

Dark Visor was too preoccupied to notice the cunning glint in Princess Liar's eyes. Over her shrieks of protest, he gave out his orders. Moments later, the droids were inside an escape pod, tumbling toward the sands of Toonilooni.

Doe Raymefar glared at Sola Teedoe.

"Well," he observed bitterly, "this is another fine mess you've gotten us into . . ."

CHAPTER TWO

Droids in Danger!

Toonilooni.

A planet of sand and sun and sun. Most people thought this was a misprint, but it wasn't. Toonilooni had two suns; one for daytime and one for nighttime (this meant there never was a nighttime, which confused everyone, especially the desert owls, who had taken to wearing wraparound shades).

So the perfect slogan for the Toonilooni Tourist Agency would have been:

Toonilooni – Planet of sun and sand (and sun).

But there was no Toonilooni Tourist Agency, because no one in their right mind (or left mind, if you were a Zargian) would ever want to visit Toonilooni. It was not only a planet of sun and sand (and sun), it was a planet of killing, maiming, gambling, and other nasty words ending in “ing.” In short, it was a planet not to be visited if at all possible.

Another perfect tourist slogan would have been:

Visit Toonilooni before you die!

This was because it was common knowledge that if you ever did visit Toonilooni as a tourist, you *would* die. You might last a couple of hours under the sun (and sun), but eventually the Jaffas, the Gutts, the Hots, the Grubbas, the Bashas, or any of the other nasty life forms that lived on Toonilooni would get to you and your valuables.

It was onto this planet that the two droids climbed out of their escape pod.

Doe Raymefar stared at the sun-bleached desert sand dunes. “I don’t suppose you brought any sunscreen with you, did you, you stupid little garbage truck?” he snapped at his droid companion before putting his hand to his mouth. “I do beg your pardon for my uncouth language, you useless, outsized baked-bean can! Oops, sorry.”

“Dweep, dweep, dweep,” dweeped Sola Teedoe.

“What do you mean, we’re back on this planet again?” asked Doe Raymefar. “We’ve just arrived.”

“Dweeeeeeeeeeep!”

Doe Raymefar looked shocked. “You mean we’ve

actually been here before, but the reader isn't supposed to know until the sequel comes out?"

"Dweep," nodded Sola Teedoe.

"I wish these authors would make their minds up," sneered Doe Raymefar. He began to walk across the hot sands. After a few moments he stopped and began to scratch himself. "I think I've got sand in my parts."

"*Hih hih hih*" snickered Sola Teedoe.

"Shut up, or I'll fuse your circuit boards with your electrodes, and you wouldn't like that, you little numskull . . ."

Sola Teedoe stopped snickering.

"Oh dear, I am sorry," apologized Doe Raymefar, "It must be the heat. Oh well, I suppose it can't get any worse . . ."

And that was when the Jaffas turned up in a huge scrap-metal van . . .

Doe Raymefar gave an electronic sigh. "It just got worse."

The Jaffas were known as being the best used-goods salesbeings in the universe. They had even been known to sell Gazumpas to the backward tribe of the Sapmuzag (and that was thought to be impossible). They were especially good at selling secondhand droids. And they didn't care how they obtained them.

Doe Raymefar stared at the small hunched figures that rushed out of the scrap-metal van. The Jaffas stared at the two droids. Their orange eyes glowed with excitement, and they rubbed their hands together.

"We must be extra polite to these people, otherwise we could be in trouble," Doe Raymefar whispered to Sola Teedoe. "Leave this to me." He turned to the Jaffas. "What are you staring at, you big ugly bunch of double-dealing, dishonest scumbags? Let me tell you this, I think you should go and stick your . . ."

A Jaffa peacemaker shot a bolt of electroforce, and Doe Raymefar was unable to finish his sentence.

If Toonilooni was the roughest, toughest planet in the solar system of Qwertyuiop, then its capital, Mos Getoutahere, was the roughest, toughest spaceport in the entire universe. All the cities on Toonilooni were pretty rough: Mos Begoin, Mos Run, Mos Dash and Mos Yuduthatathedinnertable all had terrible reputations. But Mos Getoutahere was BAD, with a capital B, A, and D.

And of all the baddest bars, in all the baddest spaceports on all the baddest planets, in all the baddest solar systems, the baddest bar in Mos Getoutahere was Riks.

The customers in Riks were a colorful bunch. Literally. There were more colors in Riks Bar than there were colors of the rainbows of the technicolor planet Barf.[1] Riks was a hangout for the down-and-outs, the up-and-ins, and inside-outs.

Chilli the Hot was sitting at the bar. He downed a glass of Toonilooni Sunsunrise (a local specialty) and

[1]323 at the last count, although this changes every time someone has a takeout pizza.

turned to watch the band that was just beginning to play. Chilli stared at the band and then at his empty glass. There was a brief pause before he began to scream. "Aaarrghhhh! I'm having hallucinations! I just thought I saw a small blue elephant playing the drums! I swear I'll never have another drink!"

"Pipe down, Chilli," grunted Dorify, the owner of Riks. She nodded toward the band. "There *is* a small blue elephant playing the drums. And a pink one playing the trumpophone."

Chilli sighed with relief. "In that case, I'll have another Sunsunrise with a dash of rocket propellant."

"Puke!" Dorify shouted. "Get your butt in here!"

Within seconds, a sallow-faced youth dressed in a white linen smock bounded into the bar. It was Puke Moonwalker.

"What you been doin', Puke, you lazy good-for-nothin'?"

"Sorry, Aunt Dorify, I was working on my Rodracer out back," answered Puke. "It's the drag races next week. I gotta beat Shebang the Hoel so I can cut loose from this life of slavery at this bar and head for the stars."

"You call it slavery," spat Dorify, "Haven't I brought you up by the sweat of my brow and the grease of my elbows? Haven't I been like a mother to you?

"You keep stopping my allowance, if that's what you mean," replied Puke bitterly.

"Shuddup, you loser. Stop dreaming and mix me a

Sunsunrise Head Banger for this customer." She nodded toward Chilli. "And go easy on the liquid nitrogen."

Puke mixed the lethal cocktail (adding the liquid nitrogen very, very carefully). Chilli gulped it down. There was a pause as his eyes (all five of them) bulged wide open. Smoke began to shoot out of Chilli's ears and nose. In the blink of an eye, he fell back off his chair and onto the floor, antennae twitching.

Aunt Dorify turned back to Puke. "Quit playing with your dumb Rodracer on my time. Get over to the Jaffas' showroom and buy a new bar droid to help me out. I'm rushed off my feet."

She *must* be busy, thought Puke as he glanced down at his adoptive aunt's nineteen feet.

An hour later, Puke arrived at the Jaffas' large glass showroom. As he entered, he glanced around at the signs lining the wall.

Droids! Droids for sale! They're going beep!

Just in! Secondhand handy droids with sixteen hands!

Hemmadroids at rock-bottom prices!

"Can I help you, sir?" A Jaffa salesbeing slid over and smiled the smile of all salesbeings everywhere. The Jaffa's orange eyes burned brightly at the prospect of a sale.

"Yes, you can," replied Puke." I need a droid."

"Well sir, may I just say that you've come to the right place," smarmed the Jaffa. "I've got droids coming out of my ears!"

"They must be very small droids."

"Oh, very good sir, small droids coming out of my ears! What a joker you are," said the Jaffa thinking something unprintable. "Follow me sir," he went on. "I've got the perfect droid for you. Just in today."

The Jaffa shuffled over to a droid perched against a wall. "What about this one, sir? A lovely model, low mileage, low maintenance, only one owner."

Puke eyed the droid. "Does it talk?"

"Talk, sir? Talk?" The Jaffa laughed. "Of course it talks: all known languages and some that haven't been invented yet. I'll show you . . ." The Jaffa took out a screwdriver and stuck it in the droid's ear.

" . . . head where both the suns don't shine!"

There was a pause as Doe Raymefar blinked and tried to come to terms with where he was and why two pairs of eyes were staring at him in wonder. "What are you staring at, wimp?" snapped Doe Raymefar.

The salesbeing laughed. "Don't worry about that, sir. It's only a malfunctioning politeness chip, nothing that can't be fixed with a lightbeam screwdriver and a sonic sledgehammer," the Jaffa said pointedly.

Doe Raymefar changed his tone immediately. "Oh dear, I do apologize, I seem to be a little disoriented! One minute I was in a desert and now I seem to be somewhere else, I don't know, how can . . ."

Puke listened as Doe Raymefar rambled on. It was strange – there was no way he would ever buy this droid, but he began to feel an affinity toward it. It was as if he and the droid were connected in some mysterious way.

" . . . and I'm sure that little runt is here too . . ." Doe Raymefar looked around the room. "Yes! There he is!" He pointed to Sola Teedoe, who was propped up underneath one of the hemmadroids.

The Jaffa was starting to smell a very good deal. "I could offer you a bargain price if you took the two droids, sir."

Puke shook his head. He pointed at Doe Raymefar "No, I'll just take this one."

Very good, sir. I'll just go get my price list." The Jaffa moved toward his computerminal.

Doe Raymefar moved toward Puke and whispered, "Would you please take my friend too? We've been through so much together . . ."

"I only need one droid," replied Puke.

"Don't make me angry, sir." The droid picked up an inch thick steel bar and casually tied it into a bow around Puke's neck. "You wouldn't like me when I'm angry . . ."

Puke gulped. He turned and called out to the salesbeing "I'll take the little one too!"

CHAPTER THREE

Ah-harr in the Bar

Next day an old, leathery-skinned spacefaring man came limping to the bar door, dragging a large, battered spaceship chest. He had an eye patch and a steel leg, and he was singing an old space shanty:

"Fifteen droids on a deactivated droid's upper body cavity,
Yo ho ho and a bottle of silicon lubricant . . ."

The old spacer hopped over to Puke, who was sweeping the bar step. "What be your name, lad?"

Puke told him.

"Well, look 'ee here, Puke lad," leered the old rascal. "Ye can bring me a double woppaburger with fries and a bottle of Maxigrog . . ." He suddenly reached out and grabbed Puke by the front of his tunic, dragging the young man closer. "And see here, matey . . ." the old spacedog glanced fearfully to the left and right, "do 'ee tell me if ye see a man in black, wearing a mask and a black cloak, who breathes like this – ***'Hurrr'haaa, Hurrr'haaa, Hurrr'haaa'*** – and yer old shipmate'll make it worth yer while. That he will. Ha ha, ah-harr, matey!"

"Yes, sir," said Puke, nervously.

"You'n me'll get on fine," growled the old man. "Take hold of my chest, lad."

After a moment, the old man said, "I meant my spaceship chest, matey."

"Oh, sorry."

Puke let go of the old spacefaring man, who stumbled into the bar, leaving Puke to struggle with his luggage.

After seeing the old spacer to his room, Puke skulked miserably into the bar.

Doe Raymefar looked up from polishing glasses. "Can I get you anything, sir?" he asked. "You pointless pile of Nwar Nwar droppings."

Puke glared at him. "Are you sure you're a diplomatic droid?"

"Of course I'm sure." The droid gave an evil cackle. "Only, I've got this malfunctioning politeness chip. You may have noticed, jelly-for-brains." He flicked an olive at Sola Teedoe.

The little droid quivered angrily. "Sagnragnrass-nfassn . . . beep . . . rickrasardly!"

Raymefar shook a mechanical fist. "Go ahead, ya rust-eaten heap of junk, blame me for everything!"

"Ssiginfigindipstik . . . beep . . . *Hih hih hih hih* . . ."

"Yeah, and the same to you, one-eye!" The enraged diplomatic droid began to hurl bottles and cocktail shakers at Sola, who retaliated by zapping Raymefar with an electronic prod.

Puke waded in to stop the furious droids from damaging each other. "Hey, cut that out!"

Suddenly, a well-aimed swizzle stick seemed to stop the little droid in its tracks. Sola became still. A panel on his body flipped open to reveal a keypad, and a well-modulated female voice floated up from his mini-speaker system.

"Welcome to the Droidaphone mail service," the voice said. "To hear a secret message from Princess Liar Origami to Oblah-Dee Oblah-Dan, Jello Knight, please press 'one.' To access the plans to the BADDIES' dreadful new secret weapon, please press 'two' . . ."

Puke was no longer listening. "Did he just say Princess Liar Origami?" he breathed in wonder. "I've seen her on the tri-vee. She's a babe. And she's loaded." He gave a little smile of pure greed. "And if she's sending secret plans, what's in this little droid's memory could be worth a fortune!"

"Aye, that it is, Puke lad," rasped a soft voice behind him.

Puke gave a squeak of alarm and spun around. Standing behind him was the old spacefaring man. He pressed the muzzle of a laser gun into Puke's suddenly knotted midriff.

"That message is for me. Oblah-Dee Oblah-Dan – only these days I calls meself Old Dan. Ye wouldn't be thinkin' o' stealin' them plans from Old Dan, would 'ee?"

Puke shook his head hurriedly.

"Good lad. 'Cause if ye were, I might be forced to fill 'ee full o' photons – purely as a matter o' business, and no hard feelin's." He thrust the gun into his belt. "Come on, Puke lad, and bring them droids. There's someone I want ye to meet."

The old man led Puke and the droids to a quiet booth at the back of the bar. Already sitting there were a shifty-looking human and a huge hairy creature that growled menacingly as they approached.

The human gave Puke a steely glance and nodded slightly. "Hans Zup."

Puke reached for the ceiling.

A look of pain crossed the other man's face. "No, that's my name," he explained wearily.

"Oh." Puke lowered his arms, feeling foolish.

Hans Zup indicated the huge hairy being. "And this is my partner, Choccibikki. He's a Cookie. He's strong and he's mean."

"Ooooarrrrgghhhhhuuuurrrggghhh," agreed the

Cookie, biting a chunk out of the table for emphasis.

Old Dan lowered himself into the seat next to Hans Zup. An urgent whispered conversation took place, during which Zup glanced at Puke, and at the small droid peeking nervously from behind his legs.

"Okay," Hans drawled. "If these plans are all you say they are, they ought to be worth megabucks – to the GOODIES, or to the BADDIES." He threw back his head and laughed. Then he signaled to Choccibikki, who grabbed Puke and tucked him under one great hairy arm.

Puke was half-smothered in fur. "What are you going to do to me?" he quavered, fighting for breath.

Old Dan grinned from ear to ear. "We be goin' to kidnap 'ee."

At that moment, Aunt Dorify's pet octopooch trotted out from behind the bar in search of things to scrounge. It stopped dead when it saw the giant Cookie, backed away as fast as its tentacles could carry it, and began to bark hysterically. Choccibikki roared at it.

Aunt Dorify came sailing out. "Toto! Toto! Stop it!" She slapped the huge hairy creature with her apron. "You ought to be ashamed of yourself, scaring a poor little thing like that."

To Puke's amazement, the Cookie dissolved into floods of tears, punctuated by whines and grunts, which Doe Raymefar translated with relish: "'Watcha do that for? I wasn't doin' nothin' . . .'"

Puke gazed at the sobbing monster. "I thought this

guy was supposed to be tough."

Old Dan rolled his eyes in exasperation. "Well, y'see, Puke lad, that's the way the Cookie crumbles."

Aunt Dorify's eyes narrowed. "Hey! Where are you takin' Puke?"

Puke turned a pleading gaze on her. "Aunt Dorify! They're kidnapping me! They're going to drag me halfway across the Galaxy to face terrible dangers and untold hardships!"

His aunt brightened up at once. "You won't be needing your room any longer, then?"

As Puke gazed at her in shock, he realized that the bar had gone quiet. A foul smell seeped into every corner of the room. In the silence, Puke heard a slithering sound, and a rumbling laugh.

"Ho, ho, ho."

Hans groaned and reached for his gun. "Something tells me that ain't Santy Claus."

A bloated shadow fell across the little group. Puke looked up into the vile and merciless features of Grabba the Gutt. Behind the crime lord's gross, and sluglike body stood the ruthless bounty hunter, Bobbi Sox, laser rifle at the ready. Behind him came a small army of Grabba's hired assassins.

"Hurrr'haaa, Hurrr'haaa, Hurrr'haaa!"

Old Dan blanched. "And it's not time for trick or treatin', so that means it must be . . ."

From the other side of the bar, flanked by Stomptroopers, strode the terrible figure of Dark Visor.

CHAPTER FOUR

Dirty Tricks at Riks

Puke stared at the figure of Visor. He felt a sudden inexplicable urge to play baseball with him.

"What have we here?" snarled Visor.

Or maybe go camping, thought Puke. He shook his head to clear it. Just as suddenly as it arrived, the feeling was gone.

"Er, Dan," stuttered Puke, "you know you asked me to tell you if I ever saw a man in black, wearing a mask and a black cloak, who breathes like . . ."

"Hurrr'haaa, Hurrr'haaa Hurrr'haaa," breathed Visor.

"Yes, just like that . . ."

"Aye, lad," replied Dan

"I think I've just spotted him. He's over there."

"You don't say, lad," said the old man, eyeing Visor like a rabbit watching a snake.

"And in case you hadn't noticed," continued Puke, "the fat blob over there is Grabba the Gutt, and he's not very nice at all. Good evening, Mr. Grabba!"

Grabba didn't answer. He watched warily as Visor moved forward.

"My old master, Oblah-Dee Oblah-Dan!" growled the Dread Lord. "What are you doing here?"

The old space pirate gave a sickly grin. "Oh I just be passin' through, Dark, just passin' through," he wheedled, touching his forelock. "And what brings ye to these parts, if I might be so bold to ask?"

"I am after certain information, and I believe that I can find it in this vicinity . . ." He stared around the room before his unforgiving eyes rested on Sola Teedoe.

Old Dan shuffled over to Visor. "Lookee here, Dark, I'll cut ye a deal. For a small price I may be able to help ye locate what ye're lookin' for."

"I do not need your help, old man. Now stand aside, or I will finish what I began years ago. Don't make me cut off your other leg."

The Dread Lord turned his back on Dan and began to

give orders to the Stomptroopers.

Instantly Dan's hand dropped to his side. With a deft flick, he yanked his steel leg from its socket and pointed it toward Visor.

VERZANG!

Puke's mouth dropped open. Dan's leg was a Power Sword! The weapon of the Jello Knights, legendary Masters of the Source and Guardians of the Peace of the Universe. Puke stared reverently at the frantically hopping figure: Old Dan, a Jello Knight?

VERZUNG!

In the blink of an eye, Visor had spun around to block Dan's unbalanced swing with his own Power Sword. Before Puke's astonished eyes, the Lords of the Source prepared to meet each other in a titanic struggle. Their Power Swords glowed with the energy of exploding stars.

VERZANNNGGGGgggg . . .

Dan's sword gave out. He looked at it closely and gulped.

"Dammmnee and tarnations," he wailed. "Low battery power. I knew I should've recharged it."

"Hurrrr'haaa, Hurrr'haaa, Hurrr'haaa." Visor began to advance on the hopping figure smiling at him inanely.

"Ha ha! Just kiddin', Dark, just kiddin'! Can't ye take a joke? You always used to be able to take a joke," whined Dan unconvincingly. "I'll just be puttin' my leg back on and usin' it to scoot out o' here, an' you can have the droids and whatever else ye might be wantin' . . ."

But Grabba the Gutt slid over toward Visor. "***Ho, ho, ho. Noahaway murthaw smibharkyard Visor. Ho, ho, ho!***"

Dan moved quickly out of Visor's reach.

The Dread Lord looked bemused. "What did he say?" asked Visor.

Doe Raymefar stepped forward. "Excuse me, Mr. Dread Lord, Dark Visor, sir, I think I might be of assistance. Allow me to translate . . ."

Visor motioned "go ahead" with his hand.

"Mr. Grabba wishes to tell you that the planet Toonilooni is his territory and therefore there is no possibility that he will allow you to take anything away from this bar, or indeed this planet. You big dollop of comet-slime," the droid added for good measure.

Visor began to breathe heavily. "Tell him that this is my property. It belongs to me. I will have it."

Doe Raymefar relayed Visor's message, and added the fact that Grabba was the spitting image of something that had come from the armpits of the Fatboy Fleas of the Moon of Phartipoop.

Grabba was none too pleased. "***Spinnonitazzz-whowl! Ho ho ho!***"

"In that case, fat face, the Great Grabba will have to blast you into little pieces."

VERZUNG!

With a deft downward stroke, Visor brought his Power Sword down onto the tip of Grabba's tail and cut it right off!

"How How How!"

Within milliseconds Grabba's henchthings and the Stomptroopers were firing at each other. Puke, Dan, and the droids huddled under a table trying to avoid the colored bolts of electroforce. They were quickly joined by the quaking Cookie.

Momentarily maddened with fear, Hans launched himself into the arms of the giant dark figure next to him. He gripped Dark Visor's neck in a terrified choke-hold. "Mommy!" he screeched.

"I don't think so!" With a contemptuous shrug, the Dread Lord threw the quivering pilot to the floor. He pointed an imperious finger. "Don't move, Hans Zup!"

Immediately all the Stomptroopers and Grabba's henchmen flung up their arms. Their weapons crashed to the ground.

Dan seized the opportunity with both hands and one leg. "Run!" he shouted. Puke, Sola Teedoe, Hans Zup, and the Cookie followed the madly hopping Dan out of the bar door before anyone could stop them.

"No!" screeched Visor. "Pick up your weapons, you fools!"

The Stomptroopers obeyed and began scrabbling around the floor for their guns.

"You imbeciles!" cried Visor. "I didn't say 'hands up,' I said 'Hans Zup'!"

There was another crash of weapons.

"Not again," moaned the Dread Lord pitifully.

By the time Dark Visor and his men had disengaged from the fight with Grabba's forces and piled out onto the street, the fugitives were nowhere to be seen.

CHAPTER FIVE

You're Bugging Me

The fleeing group screeched into one of Mos Getoutahere's many space hangars. Before them stood an excuse for a spaceship that seemed to be held together by rust and wishful thinking.

Puke gaped at the rotting hulk that stood before him.

"We're going to escape in that?" he gasped.

"Sure are, kiddo," smiled Zup proudly. "*The Millennium Bug*; fastest ship this side of the Snicker Galaxy."

"Oh?" Puke looked dubious. "How many ships *are* there this side of the Snicker Galaxy?"

"Just this one," said Hans with a mad grin. "Let's get

out of here double-pronto."

"Wait!" cried Puke, glancing around in consternation. "Where's my droid? Doe Raymefar?"

Sola Teedoe beeped and shook in an agitated manner.

Old Dan scratched his head. "I think he said, 'Let's go before we find out.'"

"He must have been caught by Dark Visor." Puke thrust out his weak chin. "We have to go back and rescue him."

Hans gazed at Puke in amazement. "Why?" he asked

Puke gave him a hard stare. "Because we don't leave our droids in there."

"Puke, we're talking *Doe Raymefar* here."

Puke thought for a moment, then said, "*Generally speaking*, we don't leave our droids in there, but in this case, we could make an exception . . ."

He followed Zup and the Cookie up the boarding ladder into the heart of the spaceship. He was quickly followed by Sola Teedoe and Dan. The doors creaked shut behind them.

Zup dived into the pilot's seat. Choccibikki took the seat next to him and began pressing buttons and pulling levers.

"Computer, get us out of here!" shouted Zup, hitting several buttons on the ship's console.

A metallic voice drifted through the ship's speaker system. "Oh, and a big hello to you too," grumbled the computer. "It doesn't take a second to say, 'Hello, how are you and have you had a nice day?' does it?"

Zup scowled. “All right, all right! Hello, how are you and have you had a nice day?”

“Since you ask, no, it’s been a . . .”

“Just get us out of here!” Zup yelled. Choccibikki roared in agreement.

“Say ‘please,’” insisted the computer.

“I will not say ‘please,’” shouted Zup. “Get us out of here NOW!”

“Temper, temper, temper! I think we’ll just sit here until someone remembers his manners.” And with that the *Millennium Bug*’s power shut off.

At the same moment, a squad of Stomptroopers hurtled into the hangar and began firing at the *Bug*.

Dan and Puke looked fiercely at Zup, who sat with his arms folded and lips pursed.

“Say ‘please’ and let’s get out of here, matey, or we’ll end up looking like frazzled lumps of Yarg meat at an Ozziman’s barbecue,” growled Dan.

“Will not!” Zup said petulantly.

Dan stared pointedly at Zup. His eyes shone with a strange light.

Suddenly, Hans’s eyes glazed over. Very slowly, he began to speak. “I’m – very – sorry – computer. Have – you – had – a – nice – day – and – please – would – you – let – us – take – off – now – if – that’s – not – too – much – trouble – for – you – thank – you – so – much – please – please – please.”

The ship’s power snapped back into life.

Puke was amazed. Here was a real live display of a

Jello Knight's power! He moved over to Dan. "Incredible," he enthused. "Were you using the legendary power of the Source, whereby you can turn minds and make people obey your every wish just through telepathic communication?"

Dan looked at Puke, puzzled. "No, lad. I was using the power of a laser pistol stuck in his left ear 'ole."

"That's better," trilled the computer happily. "Now, before we go, I just need to check that everyone has fastened their seat belts."

An explosion rocked the side of the ship.

Dan shot forward to the main computer terminal. His voice had more than a touch of titanium about it. "Listen here, compy boy, if you don't get us away in the shaking of two bells, I'll splice your mainframe and shiver your transistors. Make it yo ho ho so!"

The computer was stubborn, but not stupid. "Um, okay, there's no need to be so aggressive. I was just about to get us going. Hold on to your bits . . ."

Dark Visor stood outside the hangar and watched the *Bug* shoot off. He was annoyed, but undismayed. He might not have the plans, but he still had the Princess. She would reveal where the Rebel base was, once he got her to the Moon of Doom™. He would get the truth out of her there . . .

His gaze traveled to the silent figure standing dutifully beside him. *And now*, he thought, *I have another card to play . . .*

"Set a course for Alcapone," ordered Dan. "The sooner we get there, the sooner we get the gold stuff, doubloons, pieces of ten . . .

"Pieces of ten? I thought they were pieces of eight?" Puke queried.

"That be inflation for 'ee, lad."

"I suppose you'll take all the money and bury it on some desert asteroid and make a map and come back for it years later," said Puke.

Dan stared at Puke. "Don't be stupid, lad. I'll spend it all! Every last bit of it – on all sorts of things that'll make an old spacedog happy! So hurry up, Zup!"

"Course set and message received. Get ready for superduperhyper speed."

Zup and Choccibikki made some final adjustments to the *Millennium Bug's* navigation program.

"Here we go NOW!" Zup hit a big red button.

There was a long pause.

And then another even longer one.

"NOW!" Zup hit the button again.

Nothing.

Zup began to drum his fingers. "I'm waiting," he hissed at the computer.

He waited. So did the rest of the crew.

Eventually Zup broke the silence. "Well," he smiled feebly, "maybe we'll take our time, take in some sights and enjoy the ride. There's no need to rush – after all, Alcapone isn't going anywhere . . ."

As the *Millennium Bug* spluttered through space at the speed of an interstellar golf buggy, Puke sought out Old Dan.

"Was Visor telling the truth?" asked Puke. "Are you really Oblah-Dee Oblah-Dan, Jello Knight?"

Dan smiled a salty spacedog smile. "That I be lad, that I be."

"I've heard so much about Jello Knights, but I never thought I'd ever see one."

"Here I be in full glory. Well, most of me," Dan reached down and rubbed his metal leg.

"And are you really a Master of the Source?" asked Puke.

Dan nodded.

"But what is the Source?"

"'Tis everything, Puke lad. 'Tis the greatest power in the Universe. 'Tis an energy field that is created by all living things. But it has an Upside and it has a Downside."

"Visor had a Power Sword too," mused Puke. "Is he a Jello Knight?"

Dan looked sad. "Was, lad, was. He ain't no more. He went over to the Downside. I tried to stop 'im, but alas and alackaday, I couldn't. And this was my reward." Dan pointed to his leg.

"Visor 'ad me leg off!"

"Visor did that to you?" Puke was outraged.

"Aye, lad, that he did. Well, 'twere either Visor or a great white spacewhale, I can't remember for sure. I was drinkin' a bit too much grog at the time."

"Why did Visor turn to the Downside?" asked Puke.

Dan shook his head. "'Tis not a story for your young ears, lad."

"Please tell me," begged Puke.

"No." Dan's voice was set. "And that is my final word on the matter."

At that moment Hans Zup breezed into the cabin. "You two chewing the fat?" he asked. "Hey Dan, have you told Puke the story about his dad being a Jello Knight and you being his best buddy and Visor ratting on his dad and turning to the Downside and all that?"

There was an awkward pause. Dan stared photon bombs at Zup.

"Er, no, I guess you haven't," shrugged Zup. "I'll be on my way, then. I've got to desalinate the phase couplings – you know how it is, busy busy busy . . ."

The awkward pause continued before Puke finally broke the silence.

"Is what Hans just said true?"

Dan said nothing. Tears welled up in Puke's eyes. "I never knew my father," he whispered. "My aunt Dorify told me he sold encyclopedias."

"That was to protect ye, lad. But I knew your father, all right. Many, many moons ago. And it's true what Zup said – he was a Jello Knight like me."

Old Dan pulled a frayed travel pouch toward himself and rummaged inside. "A Jello Knight has few personal possessions, Puke lad. But your dad gave me something for ye. Something I've kept safe for many years, knowin' that one day, when the time was right, I would give it to ye. Here, lad. This is rightly yours . . ." Dan took a small cylindrical object out of the pouch and gave it to Puke.

Puke took it and gazed at its shining metal surface in awe. "My father's Power Sword!" he whispered.

"No, lad. That's his thermos. *This* is his Power Sword . . ."

Dan handed Puke a grubby-looking Power Sword. "It got a little burnt in your father's final battle."

Puke took the sword. "What do you mean, his final battle?" he asked.

"I'm sorry to tell ye, Puke lad. Your father was killed by Dark Visor. That man dressed in black with the raspy voice, that ye met today."

Puke choked back a sob. "Visor killed my father?"

"'fraid so, lad."

"Then let the whole Galaxy know that I hereby take a most sacred vow." Puke held the Power Sword close to his heart. "I, Puke Moonwalker, will avenge my father's death," he went on through gritted teeth. "I swear that I will destroy Dark Visor. I will follow him to the ends of the Universe, to the last breath of my body, to the last drop of my blood . . ."

"Er, Puke lad," interrupted Dan, "you ought to know something about Visor afore ye start carryin' on like that. He's the most powerful man in the Galaxy. He can choke the life out of your body without even touching you, and leave you an empty husk, broken like a doll. He can hurt you in more ways than any man should ever know, or imagine. He can call upon the power of the Universe and crush you so that every nerve in your body will scream out in agony and ask to die, just to be rid of the pain . . ."

There was a long pause.

Puke shrugged with elaborate unconcern. "Oh, well, I'm not the kind to hold a grudge – let bygones be bygones, I say . . . He probably had his reasons . . ."

Old Dan stood up. "Aye, well, time's a-gettin' on. Let's see what this message from young Princess Liar is all about, eh, matey?"

He led the way to the *Bug*'s conference room.

CHAPTER SIX

Bad Day for Alcapone

The motley crew of the *Millennium Bug* sat expectantly around the chipped Formica conference table. Dan gave Sola Teedoe an ingratiating leer. "Would ye care to play the Princess's message for Old Dan, matey?"

For a machine with no face, the little droid managed to do a good job of looking defiant. "Jussutryitbussa . . . beep . . . *Hih hih hih hih* . . ."

Old Dan's smile broadened. He leaned closer to the little robot. "Or would ye prefer to have Old Dan pull all yer diodes out one by one an' make ye eat them?"

Beeping with alarm, Sola Teedoe flipped open his keypad compartment. Dan pressed the number one with a grimy finger, and Liar's message floated through the *Millennium Bug*'s cabin.

"Hi, Dan – was that the tone? Drat, I hate these things – er, right, message for Oblah-Dee Oblah-Dan – oh, you know that part – er, look, Dan, my ship is not under attack. I don't want you to deliver the plans for the Moon of Doom™, which are not in this little droid's memory banks, to Alcapone. Of course, Alcapone is not the secret headquarters of the GOODIES, so there'd be no point in delivering the plans there, even if they existed, which they don't . . ."

Dan gave Puke an apologetic glance. "Ye see, matey," he said as Liar's voice rattled on in the background, "people from Alcapone are very honest and upright, so they never tell lies. But Princess Liar, ye see, was brought up to be a politician . . ."

". . . so you couldn't deliver them, even if they were in this little droid's memory, which they aren't – did I say droid? What droid? I don't see any droid . . ."

"So o' course," Dan went on, "they had to train her how to tell lies; and now she couldn't tell the truth about anything to save her life." He sighed wistfully. "A girl after me own heart, so she is."

" . . . so there's really nothing to worry about – er, that's it. See you – er, ciao – er – yes. Bye." Liar's voice trailed off into an embarrassed silence.

Puke's forehead furrowed in concentration. "So what

she really meant was . . ."

Old Dan leaped to his feet and capered with glee. "What she meant was, here's a nice little investment for Old Dan's retirement, for him to sell to the highest bidder."

Puke looked doubtful. "But she said not to take the plans to Alcapone, which means she *wants* . . ."

"Oh, we'll take 'em to Alcapone, never fear," chuckled Old Dan. Then his eyes became flinty with greed. "And if the GOODIES ain't prepared to pay a fair price for 'em – there's always the Emperor."

Hundreds of Stomptroopers, gleaming in their space armor, stood stiffly to attention as the Imperial Shuttle glided into the landing bay.

The Shuttle's landing ramp swung down. Trumpets blared in salute. A thousand troopers clicked their heels and presented arms with pinpoint precision as Dark Visor strode invincibly forward . . .

"Wipe your feet!"

The shrill voice came from a small man in a gray uniform who bustled through the ranks of Stomptroopers, shrieking with rage.

"Did you clean your boots before you came clomping onto my nice clean decks? I don't *think* so . . ."

The Dread Lord looked down at his scuffed boots. "Sorry," he muttered sheepishly.

"Well, 'sorry' won't make it right, will it? What's this?" The little man pointed a quivering finger. "Sand!

Your boots are full of sand! That stuff gets everywhere! What were you *thinking*?"

Dark Visor cleared his throat. "Great Wuss Tarquin," he growled threateningly, "the Emperor has sent me to take personal command of the fleet defending the Moon of Doom™ . . ."

"Well, hoity-toity!" snapped the Great Wuss. "Is that any reason to come in here flinging filth around?" His lip began to quiver. "I mean, look at the state of this battle station. Will you just look at it? I wear myself to a frazzle designing the most powerful killing machine in the history of the Galaxy, and do people take care of it? Oh no, they just leave empty chip bags lying around all over the place, and as for the rings from people's coffee cups – you just cannot get that stuff off! Honestly, it's enough to bring tears to your eyes."

"There, there," said Dark Visor, awkwardly patting the Great Wuss's quivering shoulder.

"People are so ungrateful!"

"There, there."

"After all I've done for them!" Tarquin blew his nose loudly. "It's not as if I mind blowing planets up for people, but couldn't they just try and keep the place tidy? Is that too much to ask?"

The Great Wuss suddenly straightened up and pointed accusingly at Visor. "Where's your apron?" he demanded.

The great warlord looked at him with astonishment. Then he realized what had been bothering him from the moment he stepped into the landing bay. His gaze swept over the massed ranks of Stomptroopers.

Every last one of them was wearing an apron. Some of them had frills.

Dark Visor breathed even harder than usual. "Imperial Stomptroopers are not supposed to wear anything over their body armor . . ."

"And how would they keep their nice armor shiny bright if they didn't wear something over it when they were cleaning their great big messy guns?" Before the Dread Lord could respond, Tarquin had looped an apron string around his neck and tied it under his cloak. "There! Now you won't get that lovely black outfit dirty, will you?"

The Dread Lord sighed. "Can we get started?" He clicked his fingers. Guarded by two Stomptroopers, Princess Liar came down the ramp from the Shuttle.

The Great Wuss Tarquin, Dark Visor, and Princess Liar stood in the vast control room of the Moon of Doom™.

Visor swung to face the Princess.

"Your pitiful rebellion will soon be over, Your Highness," he snarled.

The Princess's eyes blazed. "How dare you treat a Senator like this?"

Visor waved a gloved hand dismissively. "You are a Senator no more. The Emperor has already dissolved the Senate."

Liar glared at him. "No, he hasn't."

The Dread Lord towered over her. "Yes he has."

"Has not."

"Has too!"

"Has not!"

"Has . . . *will you stop doing that*?!" Dark Visor clenched his mailed fists, fighting to remain calm. "What is more, he will shortly be arriving to see this great new weapon in action."

"Won't."

Visor ground his teeth. "Will."

"Won't!"

The Dread Lord stamped his feet in fury. "Will, will, will! Will infinity times plus one and backsies!!"

Liar gazed at him calmly. Not quite under her breath, she muttered, "Won't."

Visor ground his teeth. With a supreme effort, he kept his voice level. "Before he arrives, we will hold a little demonstration. A demonstration that will prove to the whole Galaxy that resistance to the Empire is useless. Since you have refused to tell us where the Rebel base is, the first target for the Moon of Doom™ will be your own planet . . ." He flicked a switch and a section of wall slid open to reveal a huge viewscreen, in the center of which spun the planet . . . "Alcapone!"

Liar rushed forward in alarm. "But you can't! You'll kill millions of innocent people. Alcapone isn't the GOODIES base!"

"Aha," said Visor triumphantly, "but you always tell lies, don't you? You lied to me about the droids, and you've lied about everything ever since . . ."

"Have not."

"Have too . . . *will you cut that out*?!" Dark Visor drew a deep breath. "So if you say Alcapone *isn't* the GOODIES base, then Alcapone *is* the GOODIES basc!"

"Just a minute," said Tarquin thoughtfully. "She says Alcapone isn't the GOODIES base, so you think it is – but she could be lying."

"She *is* lying," snapped the Dread Lord.

"Yes, but she could be lying about lying, couldn't she? She knows you know she tells lies; so if she tells the truth, you'll think it's a lie. So when she says Alcapone isn't the GOODIES base, you think she's lying, and it is; but she may be telling the truth to make you think she's lying, so that you'll think it is when really it isn't."

Dark Visor rubbed his eyes with trembling fingers. "Just run that by me again?"

"It's very simple," Liar told him. "I might be telling the truth because you know I tell lies, so if I tell a lie you'll know it's really true, but if I tell the truth you'll think it's a lie, so if I want you to believe a lie I'd have to tell you the truth, even though we all know I can only tell lies." She beamed at him.

The Dread Lord held his helmeted head in his hands and moaned. "Just forget it. I don't care anymore. Let's just call the whole thing off."

Liar grinned. "Suits me."

Just then, the intercom buzzed. Dark Visor remained slumped in despair, and the Great Wuss Tarquin was still muttering in confusion.

"Shall I get that?" said Liar brightly.

She opened the comms channel. The head and shoulders of an Artillery Captain filled the screen. He seemed surprised to see Liar.

"Oh . . . er . . ." he said lamely, "I wanted to ask Lord Visor something."

Liar was feeling helpful. "Sure," she said. "Fire away."

"Oh." The Captain's brow cleared. "Okay." His picture faded from the screen.

Liar's eyes suddenly widened in horror. Her fingers scrabbled to re-establish the link. "No," she gasped, "I didn't mean . . ."

She was too late. A dreadful lightning bolt of pure energy shot from the station above them and hit Alcapone. A moment later, the planet was engulfed in a titanic explosion.

Liar watched as the remains of her homeworld drifted slowly past the viewscreen.

"Whoops," she said . . .

CHAPTER SEVEN

A Course in the Source

At the same moment, but many light-years away, Old Dan staggered and almost fell. A spasm of pain crossed the old warrior's face and left it looking drawn and haggard. He clutched his forehead dramatically. "I've just sensed a great disturbance in the Source," he gasped.

Hans gave him a disinterested glance, and went back to playing solitaire with a marked deck.

"I said, I've just sensed a great disturbance in the Source," repeated Old Dan, loudly.

Choccibikki gave an embarrassed-sounding growl.

"He said, 'Sorry about that,'" Hans translated, "'it

must have been the beans.'"

Puke edged closer to the old man. "Tell me more of the wonders of the Source, Oblah-Dan."

"Ah, Puke lad," said Dan, dropping his voice to a mysterious whisper, "many and subtle are the ways of the Source. It can bring down the mighty, influence the destinies of countless millions, sway the movements of stars in their courses, and fix parking tickets. Would ye like to learn the secrets of the Source, matey?"

"And be a Jello Knight like my father?" Puke's eyes shone. "I'd do anything – as long as it didn't involve hard study or heavy lifting."

"Then this is what ye need, lad." Old Dan reached into a pocket of his robe and drew out a handful of gaudily colored and shoddily printed leaflets, which he deposited in Puke's lap. Puke read:

The Oblah-Dee Oblah-Dan
Correspondence Course in the
Way of the Source

Men! Do girls laugh at your lack of mental muscle?

Do bullies kick sand in your face?

In just SIX WEEKS, the Oblah-Dee Oblah-Dan Method can turn you into a Jello Master!

Become attractive to girls! Make friends and influence people!

Leap tall buildings in a single bound!

Send ONLY $9.99 NOW for your FREE introductory pack!

Puke eyed the fly-specked fliers dubiously. "Strange indeed are the ways of the Source," he muttered.

Old Dan stood up. "Time to start your training, Puke lad."

The *Millennium Bug* continued to chug its erratic way across the Galaxy. In the burned-out vessel's Virtual Reality suite, Old Dan helped Puke into a Simulation suit. "I've set the VR computer to run the Duck Shoot program," he said, passing Puke his Power Sword. "Let's see how you do."

Puke reached up and pulled down the visor of his helmet. Immediately, a terrifying vision appeared before his eyes.

He whipped the visor up and turned accusingly to Dan. "What gives?" he snapped. "As soon as the program starts, I'm surrounded by thousands of vicious ducks, armed to the teeth with laser rifles."

"Of course," said Dan complacently. "The ducks come out shooting. Why do you think it's called a Duck Shoot?"

Puke shook his head. "And every time they zap me, I get a belt from the Sim suit? Forget it."

Old Dan shook his head sadly. "Puke, Puke, you must have faith. This is the way I was trained to become a Jello Knight. You must let your mind drift, Puke. Use your instincts. Don't think – let your feelings be your guide." He reached up to Puke's visor. "Give yourself wholly to the power of the Source."

As the visor came down, Puke felt a great sense of peace fall upon him. The Source was with him. He was invulnerable, indestructible, invincible. He ignited his father's Power Sword. He knew that the Source would guide his movements to deflect every laser bolt. He knew this with absolute certainty. His mind at one with the Universe, he waited as the ducks advanced . . .

. . . and opened fire.

Zap! zap Zapzapzapzapzapzapzaaaaaaaaaap!

Old Dan leaned back against the VR console and watched Puke leaping about as electric charges shot through his Sim suit. As Puke's cries for help echoed around the room, Old Dan gave a nostalgic sigh.

"Aye," he said, "that always used to happen to me, too."

Hans Zup stuck his head around the door. "Will you two quit foolin' around in here? We've nearly reached Alcapone."

As Hans led the way back to the control room, the *Millennium Bug* reeled under a series of ferocious hammer blows. Hans staggered into the cockpit as the ship lurched again.

"What gives?" he yelled over the shriek of alarms. "Are we under attack?" Realizing that Choccibikki was responding to the crisis by hiding under his chair, Hans turned to stare out of the cockpit windows just as Puke and Old Dan came staggering in.

Hans gave a snort of disgust. "We're in an asteroid

field. I'll have to try and fly our way out of it."

"Strange," said Dan slowly, "I don't remember any asteroid fields near Alcapone."

"Yes, but you don't remember to put your shorts on half the time," Hans told him curtly. "What do you think is hitting the ship? Marshmallows?"

"Wait," cried Puke as Hans began to turn. "What's that sign over there?" He pointed off to the left. Grudgingly, Hans piloted the *Bug* closer.

The sign, composed of ionized gas in a stasis field, read:

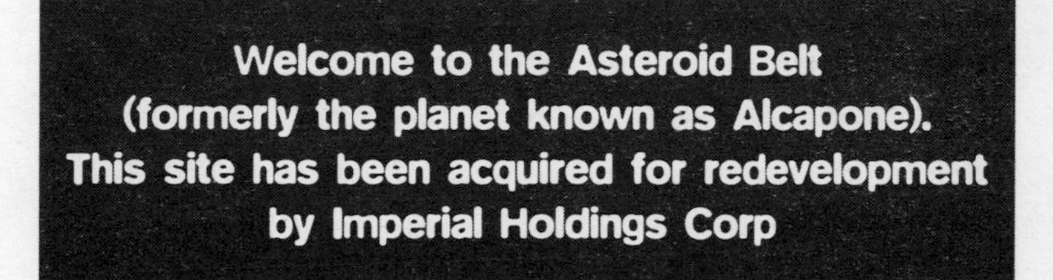

As they gazed with horror at the remains of their destination, a small ship flew out from the shelter of one of the larger asteroids. Its pilot saw the *Bug* in front of it, and the tiny ship skidded to a halt. It hovered uncertainly for a moment, then shot away at high speed.

"That be a BADDIES scout ship," said Dan.

Hans stared nervously after the retreating vessel. "Well, if it don't mess with me, I ain't gonna mess with it."

Dan shrugged. "It carries virtually no weapons."

Hans gave a whoop. "Let's get it!" He kicked his copilot in the rear. "C'mon, Chocci. It's clobberin' time!"

The *Millennium Bug* executed a clumsy turn and lumbered in pursuit.

Some time later, Puke happened to glance behind them.

"Hans," he said.

The *Bug*'s pilot was intent on his pursuit of the scout ship. "Not now, kid."

Without turning, Puke began to tug at Hans's sleeve. "Ha-aaans?"

Zup batted Puke's hand away irritably. "What is it?"

"Oh, I just wanted to check up on some basic astrophysics. You know planets?"

"Yeah?"

"Well, don't they normally sort of float in orbit around suns? I mean, they don't usually take days off and zoom around the Galaxy sightseeing, do they?"

"No – why do you ask?"

"Because there seems to be one following us. And planets usually have like continents and oceans and rivers and mountains and stuff, don't they?"

"Usually . . ." Hans was getting a terrible sinking feeling.

"They're not usually, well let's say for the sake of argument, made completely of steel and bristling with guns and radar dishes and stuff?"

"Not usually," said Hans slowly, "no."

"And they don't usually have 'Moon of Doom™' painted on the side in letters fifty miles across?"

Beads of sweat stood out on Hans's brow. "Get us

out of here, Chocci!" he yelled. "Maximum speed!"

But at that moment, the ship shuddered as a powerful tractor beam locked onto it. Engines whining uselessly, the *Millennium Bug* was drawn inexorably into the steel embrace of the Moon of Doom™.

CHAPTER EIGHT

Cunning Plans

The ***Millennium Bug***'s alarms howled despairingly.

Within moments, the highly trained crew had sprung into action. Choccibikki leaped to the locker that housed the ship's supply of deadly laser rifles, and hid in it, sobbing pitifully. Hans Zup quickly scribbled a lengthy confession. Sola Teedoe raced around in circles beeping madly.

"What are we going to do?" wailed Puke.

"Cop a plea, lad," advised Dan, busily sticking straws in his hair. "Or do what I do – pretend to be totally ga-ga."

"What's to pretend?" sneered Hans.

"*Mroooawwwwrrruuuaaaaeerrrrrr*," moaned Choccibikki from inside his locker.

Hans rolled his eyes. "No, Chocci, I don't think it would be a good idea to throw ourselves on their mercy. Anyway, I've got a better idea!"

The first squad of Imperial Stomptroopers to board the *Bug* peeked nervously through the door into the flight deck. They looked around incredulously. Then they started snickering and nudging each other.

The squad leader made hurried shushing motions and spoke into his helmet radio. "Search squad to Control. We have secured the captive ship. The crew appears . . ." the squad leader coughed hurriedly as if to cover a fit of giggles " . . . appears to be dead."

The voice of the controller, tinny and muffled, said, "Dead? What do you mean, dead? Oh . . . dead? Right."

"Yes, Control." The squad leader seemed to be afflicted with another fit of chuckling. "No sign of life here."

"Oh . . . well." The controller also seemed to be cracking up. "Well, better leave everything undisturbed, and I'll send in a couple of *unarmed* and *totally defenseless* orderlies to clean up in there."

"Right, Control," said the squad leader over the sound of his men doubling up with laughter. "We're outta here." He led his squad off the flight deck, alternately dragging and kicking troopers who were incapacitated with mirth. The sound of their footsteps and guffaws gradually faded.

The "corpse" of Puke Moonwalker sat up and shook its head. "I can't *believe* that worked." He glared at the recumbent figure of Hans. "Especially since you have that stupid rubber sword stuck under your arm." He turned to Dan. "And frankly, I don't think that bunch of lilies on your chest is fooling anybody."

Hans came to life with a snort. "What's your problem? It worked, didn't it?"

Puke still looked doubtful. "You don't think they suspected anything, do you?"

Old Dan waved a lily in admonishment. "No, matey. Not a thing."

A few minutes later, two suspiciously round-shouldered and pigeon-chested Stomptroopers limped uncertainly down the ramp from the captured ship, wheeling the "dead bodies" of Old Dan and Choccibikki on carts. Sola Teedoe followed; Hans had insisted that he wear a mourning veil for effect.

Hans and Puke had overcome the troopers sent to guard the *Bug* with surprising ease. Indeed, Puke was uncomfortably aware that the troopers had surrendered even before he and Hans had produced their concealed weapons.

Laser rifle at the ready, Hans approached the door to the control room and slapped the "open" button. With a scream of terror, he hurled himself through the doorway, firing into the room. Puke followed his example. Old Dan and the Cookie made a grab for hidden weapons and joined the fray.

After almost a minute's furious blasting, their weapons fell silent. The smoke slowly cleared.

The control room was totally empty.

On top of a half-melted computer station, Puke found a badly singed message card that read, "Out to lunch. Back later."

"That's lucky," said Puke, uneasily trying to ignore the stifled guffaws that seemed to come from somewhere nearby.

Old Dan struck a pose. Fingertips on temples, eyes crossed in concentration, he intoned, "By the power of the Source, I see that the tractor beam that brought us here is controlled from deep inside the station, where the Bridge of Peril crosses the Unfathomable Abyss of Oblivion."

Puke stared at Dan in awe. "Truly, a breathtaking display of the power of the Source,' he whispered reverently.

"Sure," said Hans caustically. "That, and the fact that the old crock just read the sign over there." He pointed to a placard on the wall which, though severely blast-damaged, still read quite legibly in letters a foot high:

INSTRUCTIONS FOR SHUTTING OFF TRACTOR BEAM:

GO DEEP INSIDE THE STATION TO WHERE THE BRIDGE OF PERIL CROSSES THE UNFATHOMABLE ABYSS OF OBLIVION. SHUT DOWN POWER SWITCH MARKED "TRACTOR BEAM."
SAFETY ADVICE: DON'T FALL OFF THE BRIDGE.

Old Dan shivered. "'Tis a desperate venture, shipmates. Who would be reckless or foolhardy enough to risk their lives on such a perilous quest?" He turned to face the others. "What be you a-lookin' at Old Dan like that for, mateys?" he quavered.

Two pairs of hands, one pair of huge hairy paws, and Sola Teedoe's gripper arm simultaneously grasped the protesting oldster and shoved him bodily through the door, which slammed behind him. When hammering, screams of defiance, and threats produced no result, Old Dan finally stumbled away to carry out his allotted task, swearing horrible curses under his paint-stripper breath.

In the control room, Puke and his companions bravely masked their concern for Old Dan's fate by playing a few rounds of *Clued-Up*.

Puke stared keenly at Hans. "I accuse Salamis the Slayer, in the Virtual Reality suite, with the Kremozian Ceremonial Backstabber."

Hans curled his lip. "Not even close, kid."

Puke shrugged and headed for the vending machine in the corner. "Anyone want a cola?" He dropped a two-credit piece into the slot. Nothing happened.

"Kick it right under the coin slot," a disembodied voice advised Puke.

"Oh, thanks." Puke did so, and the machine disgorged a bottle. Puke reached out for it. A puzzled look crept over his face.

"Did you say something?" he called over to Hans.

Hans shook his head. "Why?"

"I could have sworn I . . ." Puke's attention was suddenly caught by the contents of the bottle. Instead of a bubbly brown liquid, it appeared to hold a rolled-up piece of paper. Puke unscrewed the cap and pulled it out. It read:

To whom it may concern:

Help! I am a prisoner in Cellblock H. I am being horribly tortured, but I will never reveal the GOODIES' secrets.

Yours sincerely,

Princess Liar.

PS: All the above statements are completely untrue.

"A message in a bottle – from the Princess! She's here!" Puke rushed over to the surveillance screens and began punching buttons.

Hans, Choccibiki, and the droids watched him in astonishment. 'Who's here?" demanded Hans.

Puke was furiously channel-zapping. Scene after scene from surveillance cameras and home shopping channels flashed over the screens. "Prince Liar Origami. She's with the GOODIES. Sola Teedoe belongs to her." Puke finally managed to tap into the detention block security system and find Liar's cell. "Aha."

Hans stepped forward to look at the screen. His eyes widened as he gazed at the screen, which showed

Princess Liar reclining on a hard, unyielding lounge chair and easing her tortured spirit with a frosty piña colada and fruit bonbons.

Zup let his breath out in a low whistle. “Hubba hubba hubba, “ he crooned, “getta load of that sweet thing. Just the gal I’ve been saving myself for.”

Luke felt his blood run cold as icy streams of jealousy flooded his veins. He spun furiously to face the captain of the *Millennium Bug*.

“Back off, live wire,” he snarled, his fingers inching toward his Power Sword. “I saw her first.”

Hans reached surreptitiously for the laser equalizer at his belt. “Is that so, pipsqueak?” he rasped. “And what makes you think a classy dame like the Princess is going to go for a 4-F cop-out like you?”

“Oh, you think she’d be more interested in a know-nothing blowhard with a smart mouth, do you, Mister Fancypants?” hissed Puke spitefully.

Hans gave a mirthless laugh. “Okay, buckwheat. Why don’t we let the lady decide? You just keep your sorry butt down here, and I’ll go and rescue her . . .”

“Nix!” yelled Puke furiously. “Take a back seat, homeboy, while I do the Seventh Cavalry bit.”

They glared at each other, testosterone sloshing out of their ears.

“Tell you what, big shot,” sneered Hans, “let’s make it a race. Last one to rescue Princess Liar is a Dunniganian Slime Louse.” Pausing only to knee Puke in the breadbasket, Hans palmed the control room door open and sped down the corridor. With a slightly breathless squeak of rage, Puke followed suit.

Left alone, Choccibiki and Sola Teedoe stared at each other.

“Rassn’fassndum-dums . . . beep . . . *Hih hih hih hih,”* opined Sola.

“Woarrarwaaaarrrrraaaar,” roared Chocci in agreement.

CHAPTER NINE

Upside-Down, Downside-Up

Puke and Hans burst into the guardroom of Cell-block H, squabbling furiously. Puke held a cowering warden and his deputy at bay with his Power Sword. Hans grabbed the warden by the throat. "Okay, punk, get the keys to the Princess's cell. You keep these two on ice while I go get the lady."

Puke's sword swung toward Hans. "I got a better idea, lowlife. Why don't you keep the goons covered while *I* go get the lady."

Puke and Hans faced each other, weapons ready to deal out instant death to each other – and anyone else unfortunate enough to be in the way.

"Tell you what," said the warden tremulously, "why don't we all go and get the lady . . . ?"

As the door of her cell swung open, Princess Liar looked up with some annoyance.

Elbowing Puke savagely in the chest, Hans announced, "Okay, doll, start packing, the marines just arrived."

The Princess gave a discontented sigh. "Oh, what a bore. Could you call back later? My manicurist hasn't stopped by today."

Hans stared at her in disbelief. "Hey, sister, I'm here to rescue you from torture and worse. You ain't being taken to no garden party . . ." He broke off as a jab from Puke's elbow sent him reeling.

"Please, Your Highness. We are here to take you to Oblah-Dee Oblah-Dan," hissed Puke.

Immediately, the Princess's eyes lit up. "Oblah-Dan? Well, what are we waiting for, guys? Time to boogie on outa here!"

Leaving the relieved wardens locked in Liar's cell, the Princess and her rescuers sped away from the detention block. Puke and Hans had reached a plateau of acrimony and were not speaking to each other, so their progress was swift until they reached a junction in the corridor.

"This way," cried Puke, dragging Liar to the left.

"Are you blind?" growled Hans, hauling the unfortunate Princess to the right. "We go this way!"

"Oh, you think you're so clever! I tell you, I remember coming down this corridor . . ." Puke almost yanked Liar's arm from its socket.

Furious, the Princess snatched both arms from their grip. "Will you bozos give me a break? I'm the royalty around here, I get to choose." After a moment's thought, she stormed off down the right-hand corridor. Hans gave Puke a smirk of victory.

Puke gave an elaborate and unconvincing shrug. "Fine," he yelled at the Princess's determinedly indifferent back. "Go with the big ape. Who needs a stupid girl around anyway? See if I care. I'll just go this way by myself and wander around until the Stomptroopers get me or I die of starvation. Then you'll be sorry."

Hans raced to catch up with the Princess while Puke, wallowing in self-pity, set off alone.

Dan pressed himself back into a dark corner of Force Field Generator Room PP0907 and listened with bated breath to the footsteps of the searching Stomptroopers, hoping they would pass the door and fade away. They didn't. The door hummed open again, and two suspicious-looking Stomptroopers peered in.

"Anybody in the Force Field Generator Room?" asked one of the troopers.

Summoning all his mental abilities, Old Dan called upon the mind-controlling powers of the Source to allay the troopers' suspicion.

"No sir," he croaked, "ain't nobody in here but us

force field generators."

There was a moment's pause, and a stifled giggle. Then the inquisitive trooper said, "Oh, well, that's all right, then . . ." and the door closed.

The little room was silent except for the hum of the machines and, from outside, the sound of two heavily armored men trying to creep away on tippy-toes.

Puke stood in an open doorway in the side of a huge air shaft, uncomfortably aware that he may have taken a wrong turn. He and Hans hadn't crossed this monstrous void – he was sure he would have remembered. On the other hand, a sign on the opposite side of the shaft read:

THIS WAY TO LANDING BAY DSJ7
WHEN BRIDGE IS RETRACTED, GO AROUND

Puke eyed a projecting piece of steelwork above the opening on the far side of the shaft. He was carrying a grapple and lifeline in his utility pouch, since such items were invaluable on a world that consisted almost entirely of sand dunes. He could fire the grappling hook to latch onto the projection, and then swing over the limitless drop, entrusting his life to a thin rope, and rejoin his friends . . .

After a moment's consideration, Puke thought, "Nah!"

He turned and headed back into the bowels of the Moon of Doom™.

Princess Liar continued to stride down corridors with Hans scurrying behind her. Suddenly she held up her hand in warning. From around the corner came a low voice, muttering bitterly to itself:

"Always the way, isn't it? You get carted across the bleak infinity of interstellar space – and I'm not talking first class here – they ask you a few questions, and then what? They forget you, just leave you to wander off, who cares? I'm just another droid . . ."

Hans pushed past the Princess's restraining hand. "Hi, laughing boy. Long time no see."

Doe Raymefar raised his head sullenly. "Well, look what the cat threw up," he said derisively. "If it isn't Captain Klutz."

"Yeah, it's really average to see you, too," said Hans. "You wanna hang around here all day badmouthing people, or do you wanna hitch a ride?"

"Why, a ride would be most welcome, sir . . . Why dincha wait for me at Riks, huh?" demanded the grouchy droid. "You guys went hightailing it outta there like a bunch of spooked bunnies, never a thought for poor old Doe Raymefar . . ."

"So what happened to you?"

"They captured me." The droid's voice cracked with remembered horror. "I could tell you tales of torture and terror that would . . ."

"Save them for beddy-bye time," snapped Hans. "We ain't out of the gumbo yet." He gave Liar an ingratiating leer. "This way, cupcake."

The Princess gave him an icy glance. "I'm being rescued by a male chauvinist pig and a deranged droid. How did I ever get so lucky?"

"Don't knock it, sister," snapped Hans as Liar strode on. "You could be back in your cell waiting to be tortured!"

"Tell me about it," Liar shot over her shoulder. "I just didn't know when I was well off."

Old Dan swayed slightly as he inched his way around a tiny ledge over the Unfathomable Abyss of Oblivion. The ledge led from the Bridge of Peril around the Tractor Beam controls. It was a full three feet wide and surrounded by a substantial guardrail. Old Dan inched along it, trembling with terror and self-pity. "Oh that's right, shipmates," he growled under his breath, "any dangerous, dirty work to do, get Old Dan to do it, he don't mind don't Old Dan . . ."

At length, his questing fingers found the switch marked "Tractor Beam." Sweat streaming from every pore, Dan reached out and turned the switch to "off." Then he inched his way back along the ledge.

Sitting slumped on the Bridge of Peril, Old Dan was too exhausted to notice the approach of heavy footsteps and labored breathing until a black-clad shape stood towering over him, Power Sword at the ready.

"Guess who!" said Dark Visor.

Guards surrounded the landing bay.

Choccibikki and Sola Teedoe had evidently made a

break for the *Bug*. Hans could see them through the cockpit windows. The *Bug*'s engines were chugging, ready for takeoff. Choccibikki had his hands over his eyes.

Princess Liar eyed the *Bug* with disgust.

"Nice ship. Is the rubber band all wound up?"

Hans surveyed the situation and made a tactical decision.

"We'll never make it," he moaned.

Liar snatched the captured laser rifle out of his hands. "Cover me, chicken."

She burst into the landing bay, firing with enthusiasm and woeful inaccuracy. To Hans's astonishment, guards keeled over to left and right, even though the energy bolts from Liar's gun never came close to hitting any of them.

With a mental shrug, Hans raced for the *Bug*, with Doe Raymefar clattering after him.

"VERZANG!"

"VERZENG!"

"VERZING!"

"VERZONG!"

"VERZUNG!"

"VERZAEIOUNG!"

Old Dan wiped the sweat from his eyes with an unsteady hand and glared at Dark Visor. "Will ye for pity's sake stop making those stupid noises and just get on with the fightin'?"

The titanic battle between Dark Visor and Old Dan ranged to and fro over the Bridge of Peril. Dan's good leg was starting to buckle, but Visor's breathing was becoming ragged. By unspoken agreement, the combatants lowered their weapons for a momentary rest.

"Your strength is failing, old man," rasped the Dread Lord.

Old Dan's voice shook with the effects of exhaustion and grog. "Ye can't win, matey. If ye cut Old Dan down . . ." he hesitated " . . . well, ye'll feel terrible guilty about it in the mornin', I can tell ye,"

The Dread Lord raised his Power Sword. "Wanna bet?"

Puke, hopelessly lost, stumbled onto a balcony in the side of the Unfathomable Abyss of Oblivion, overlooking the Bridge of Peril. He gazed down and gave a cheery wave. "Hey, Dan? Have you seen the others . . .?"

Startled, Old Dan glanced up. In that moment of distraction, Dark Visor's Power Sword sliced around in a deadly arc toward the old pirate's unprotected body. With robes fluttering, Dan's body pitched over the side of the bridge and fell headlong into the Abyss.

Far above, Puke put his hand across his mouth.

"Oops."

Hans scrambled into the *Bug*'s pilot seat. "Computer, prepare for takeoff."

The computer gave an electronic snort of annoyance.

"Well, here you are at last. What time do you call this? I've been worried sick . . ."

"Never *mind*, I'll do it myself." Hans slammed the throttle open and executed a screeching handbrake turn. The *Millennium Bug* shot away from the Moon of Doom™ and out into the void.

"Where to, your lusciousness?" leered Hans.

"The last remaining GOODIES base is not on a moon of the planet Yonkers," said Liar. "We don't have to get there. It's not a matter of life and death."

"I hear what you're not saying." Hans programmed the *Bug*'s navigation computer to set a course for Yonkers.

Puke found himself in a hangar full of Imperial TOY fighters. The deadly little combat spacecraft lay in launching racks, ready for instant takeoff.

Puke turned to look out of the large window that filled one wall of the hangar. To his fury and utter disbelief, he watched the *Millennium Bug* lurch away from the station like a student driver with a blocked fuel line.

"The jerks!" he raged. "They left without me!"

Just then, the door behind Puke swung open to reveal a surprised-looking pilot. One vicious bang on the noggin and a quick change of uniform later, and Puke was at the controls of a TOY fighter, speeding away from the Moon of Doom™.

Having returned to the control bridge of the gigantic battle station, Dark Visor sat at his control console watching the ships depart. He gave a satisfied nod. His plan was working perfectly. It had been an inspiration to allow the Rebel scum to escape. They had no idea that Visor had cunningly arranged for a homing beacon to be planted on the *Millennium Bug*, in order to lead the Moon of Doom™ straight to the last remaining GOODIES base . . .

The door to the bridge sighed open, and a technician slouched in, tucking the stub of a half-finished cigarette behind one grubby ear. He held out a small device with a flashing red light on top for the Dread Lord's inspection.

"Was this the type of homing beacon you wanted planting on that Rebel ship, buddy?"

The Dread Lord lowered his helmeted head and banged it on the console in despair.

CHAPTER TEN

Mellow Jello

Puke's fighter skidded across the black void of space in a series of stomach-churning arcs. It was just like driving his Rodracer on Toonilooni. He'd never gotten the hang of that, either.

Puke's head was full of questions: Where should I go? he thought. What should I do? Will Princess Liar be attracted to me if change my deodorant?

"Puke lad . . ."

Puke looked around. There was no one else there!

"Puke." It was the voice of Old Dan! But how on Zarg could it be?

"Dan, is that you?" Puke called out. "I thought you were dead."

"Technically, I am, matey – thanks to you distractin' me just when I had that big lug on the ropes, I might add."

"Ah, yes," began Puke apologetically. "Sorry about that. I promise it won't happen again."

"Aye, well, let bygones be bygones, lad. I don't know why I be helpin' ye at all, except ye'd started my 'Become a Jello Knight Course' and I don't want ye askin' for yer money back, 'cause I've spent it already."

"So what happens now?"

Dan's voice continued to sound in Puke's mind. *"You must fulfill your destiny, lad. You must become a Jello Knight. You have to head for the planet of Jello-stone. There lives the legendary Jello Master, Yoggi. He will teach you the strange and wondrous Ways of the Source. He trained me and he trained your father and he gives very good discount rates for group bookings – plus I'll get a commission for recommending you."*

"But you're dead!" exclaimed Puke.

"Old habits dies hard, lad."

"How do I get to Jello-stone?" asked Puke. "Will you guide me there, using the mystical powers of the Source?"

"No, Puke lad. I'll guide ye there using the mystical powers of the star directory in the glove compartment. You'll find Jello-stone on page thirty-two. Oops, gotta go now, I got an incoming call from my broker on three . . ." Dan's voice faded into nothingness.

"Dan, Dan, come back!" Puke howled. But in the vastness of space no one could hear him scream.

The planet of Jello-stone lay before Puke. He glided toward the surface in a series of heart-stopping stall turns. Jello-stone was a planet of mist, swamp, small log cabins, and motor-home parks.

Puke crash-landed the fighter in a startling display of inept flying, and stepped out into a large, deep pool of water. One panicky dog paddle later, he stood dripping on the bank, taking in his new surroundings.

How will I ever find this Yoggi in this vast wilderness? he thought. Looking around the inhospitable terrain, he thought he saw a light in the distance. Wading cautiously through dark swamp water, Puke set off toward it. As he came nearer, the source of the light was revealed as a large flashing neon sign:

The flaking plywood arrows led to a clearing where a strange brown creature with large ears was sitting. It was wearing a hat, a tie, and nothing else. It saw Puke and jumped up. "Oh boy, oh boy, another tourist with a pickernick basket," it slobbered, licking its lips.

"Are you Yoggi, the Jello Knight?" asked Puke hopefully.

Within a blink of an eye, the creature's manner changed. "Yoggi indeed am I. The average Jello am I smarter than, Poo-poo."

Puke stood, trying to make sense of the Jello Knight's ramblings.

"I'm not Poo-poo. I'm Puke Moonwalker, and I've been sent to you by Oblah-Dee Oblah-Dan."

The Jello Knight nodded. "Ah, Jello training you are wanting, this way with me come."

As he followed Yoggi, Puke explained the extraordinary circumstances that had brought him to the planet of Jello-stone. The Jello Knight yawned constantly through the long story, occasionally interrupting Puke to warn him of the dangers of the swamp.

"On that low branch your head . . ."

CLUNK!

"Owwww!"

" . . . mind."

Eventually, they arrived at a tumbledown mud hut set in the middle of the swamp at the side of a sprawling beingrove tree. The house was smaller than a beaver's lodge, and a lot less tidy.

"Home, home, sweet," murmured Yoggi. "Come you in."

Puke bent down and tried to squeeze into the house. He managed to get his head and shoulders through the tiny door before he became wedged tight.

"I think, I'll just stay out here. I kind of like the outdoor life," Puke grunted.

"Yourself suit," muttered Yoggi.

"So how do I become a Jello Knight and learn the Power of the Source?"

"Ask that you may," replied Yoggi.

"I just did," replied Puke.

"Long is the path, learning of the Source, hard is the way. Ready are you for hard training long?"

Puke's mind was beginning to reel. "Er, yes, I think so. How many years did you take to train my father and Dan?"

"Years many, training your father I was. Day of every morning early, late of feeding Source is, fee large, upside is downside, outside is inside, sides there are many."

Puke was rapidly growing impatient with the old Jello Knight's verbosity. "I'm not surprised it took him years – how did he ever understand you? How long would it take you to train me if you spoke proper English?"

Yoggi scratched his head. "Oh, three or four days, maybe."

Puke gave him a hard stare. "Tell you what, let's make it two."

"Can't this crate go any faster?" yelled Liar. "They're shooting at us!"

The *Millennium Bug* shuddered from the fire of the Imperial TOY fighters that were in close pursuit.

Choccibikki put his hands over his eyes and moaned "Waroowww!"

"We're all going to die," Doe Raymefar translated. "Ya big yellow furball," he added.

"Come out from under the table and put that white flag away," Hans ordered Choccibikki.

"Do something!" shouted Liar.

"I'm trying, sweet pea! Computer, give me more power, double-quick!"

The computer's metallic voice rang out. It sounded petulant. "I'm doing my best and all you can do is shout at me. Well that's it, you're on your own. Good-bye."

Liar shook her head. "Oh, great. Terrific."

As the *Bug* skimmed over the surface of a pitted asteroid, the TOY fighters moved in for the kill.

"Hang on to your spacebeans, folks!" Hans banked the ailing ship into a wingover and shot toward the surface of a large asteroid in a suicidal power dive.

Liar stared at him in horror. "Are you crazy?"

"There's a crater dead ahead," yelled Hans. "We'll hide out there."

The *Bug* stuttered toward a vast black cavern. As they shot through the entrance, Liar gave a nervous cough. "Have we just passed a row of huge, sharp, pointy teeth?"

Hans snorted. "Just a coincidence. They're not teeth, they're just rock formations that look like teeth. Trust me."

The *Bug* spluttered on into the darkness as the "cavern entrance" suddenly snapped shut behind them.

Hans gave Liar an apologetic look. "Oops! Okay, so maybe they were teeth."

"Great rescue!" snapped Princess Liar. "Now you've got us trapped inside a giant space slug. What do you do for an encore, shoot me in the head?"

The Bug lay on its side in the slug's intestine. Corrosive slug juices washed over its hull.

"So I made a mistake," Hans snarled sullenly. "Sue me."

"Brother, you are one big turkey," muttered Liar.

Hans brightened up. "Hey – you're always lying, right? So you don't mean that. You think I'm a great guy, really."

"Hans, I think you're the biggest hunk in the Universe," said Liar pointedly.

While Hans scratched his head trying to figure that one out, Liar picked up a stellar flashlight and headed for the ship's airlock.

"Come on, let's get out there and explore."

Choccibikki began to roar. "Rooowwarrrrrr!"

"What's wrong with him?" asked Liar.

"He's afraid of the dark."

Leaving Choccibikki and the droids on the *Bug*, Liar and Hans made their way out of the ship and began to squelch along the intestinal tubes of the space slug. They moved carefully through a series of cavernous stomachs that were lined with the wrecks of half-dissolved spaceships.

As Liar and Hans entered another stomach, they heard voices. In the gloom, a group of beings were sitting next to the wreck of a large ship. Its registration began with "NCC" – the rest had been eaten away.

"What are they doing?" asked Liar.

Hans shone his light into the dark. "Looks like they're fishing. They must be trying to catch something from the gastric juices of the space slug."

"Gross."

Voices floated out of the gloom.

"Fascinating, Captain. The creature appears to have a body chemistry based entirely on playdough."

"We must try to . . . communicate with this being. If we could only . . . talk to it . . . we must . . . boost our hailing frequencies . . ."

"I cannae do it, Captain. I have nae got the poower!"

Farther away, a man in a pilot's uniform with the name "Rogers" on the shoulder was discussing the finer points of football plays with a man wearing tights and a tunic with a lightning bolt across it. In the middle distance, a flatheaded being with big eyes prodded disconsolately at what looked like a cell phone.

Liar's voice shook with pity. "Can't we help these poor people?"

Hans gave her an incredulous glance. "Are you serious?"

"No," she lied.

"Well, we can't. We'll be lucky to get out of this

ourselves." Suddenly Hans snapped his fingers. "Come on, back to the ship. I've got an idea."

Hans slid into the cockpit, with an industrial-strength electric razor hidden behind his back.

"Hey, Chocci, baby, how ya doin'?"

"Rrrrooooaaaawwwlll?"

"Do you really think this is going to work?" asked Liar, as Hans applied a match to the huge pile of fur they had shaved off the protesting Cookie.

"You better believe it, sister." Hans blew on the embers and stood up, brushing glop off his pants. "Ain't nothin' smells worse than a burnt Cookie."

"Start the engine and hang on!" roared Hans, as he sprinted for the airlock. He could barely be heard above the roar of the gastric gases and juices that were beginning to swirl around the intestines in response to the smoldering pile of Cookie fur. Sullen and shivering, the hairless Choccibikki complied.

The *Millennium Bug* began to roll and buck. Wave upon wave of mucus and phlegm washed over the *Bug*, binding it up in a green, sticky glob.

The *Bug*'s engines spluttered into life. The ship began to ride a great green tsunami of slug juice.

"Aaaaaaaaaaaaa . . . . . ."

"Hang on, people, this could be a rough ride," grated Hans.

"Aaaaaaaaaaaaaaaaaaaaaaaa . . . . . ."

"Here goes nothin'!"

"Aaaaaaaaaaaaaaaaaaaaaaaaaaaaaa aaaaa . . . . . . ACHOOOOO!"

The *Bug* shot out of the Slug's nose in a mass of sticky slug snot and mucus. Moving at a substantial fraction of the speed of light, the glop-laden ship soared messily across the void.

"Ride that big green roller!" roared Hans. "Yeee-haaaaaa!"

DOOOOOOONNNNNNGGGGGG!

The crew of the *Bug* picked themselves up off the cockpit floor, rubbing at tender bits.

Liar groaned. "What in the Galaxy did we just hit?"

Hans staggered to his feet and peered through the slime-covered cockpit window.

Through the glutinous mucus, he could see that the *Bug* was stuck fast against the side of a huge space-barge. Hans could just make out the bulk of a familiar-looking and unwelcome figure gazing out from a viewport in the barge's side.

The *Bug*'s radio system crackled into life

"Ho ho ho!"

Hans collapsed into the pilot's seat. "That's all we need – Grabba the Gutt!"

CHAPTER ELEVEN

Grabba Is Gutted

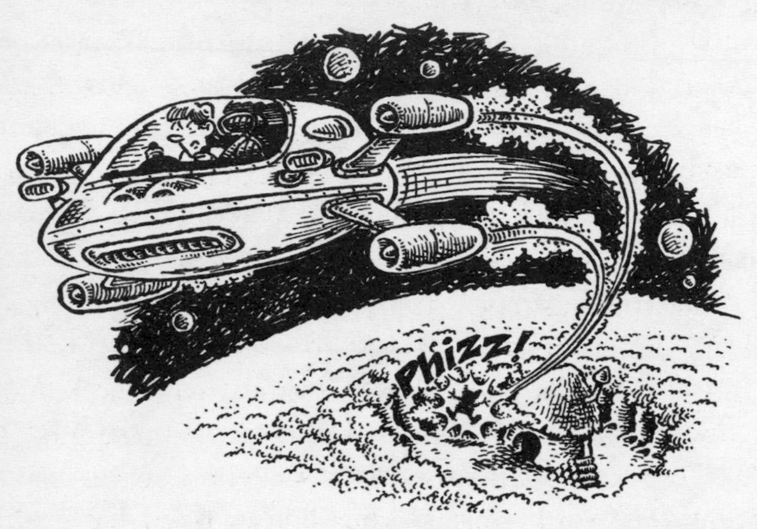

Grabba's boarding party had met with no resistance from the *Bug*'s shaken crew. Moments after their collision with the Gutt's barge, Hans, Liar, Choccibikki (wearing a nylon housecoat at least forty sizes too small and looking terminally embarrassed), and the droids stood before the sluglike figure of the evil crime lord. The Princess quailed at the sight of the obscenely bloated villain. Her fear condensed into a tight knot of terror, until it burst out in a telepathic scream for help which tore through the vastness of space . . .

"Puke! Puke! We're going to die! Help us!"

On the swamp planet of Jello-stone, Puke cocked his head as the disembodied voice shrieked in his mind. His eyes widened in shock, and he dropped the hammer he was holding – right onto Yoggi's foot,

"*Yeeeoooow!* What you are doing, mind, you big galoot!" snapped the Jello Master, sucking his aching toes.

"My friends are in trouble," cried Puke in dismay. "If I don't go to help them, they'll die!" He shrugged his shoulders. "On second thought, who cares?"

"Go, you must not!" Yoggi told him sternly. "Incomplete, your training is."

Puke glared at him. "Will you quit it with the Arnie Schwarzenbeing dialogue? Anyway, what training?" Puke checked off points on his fingers. "So far, I've swept your yard, cleaned your house, fixed the roof, and chopped enough firewood to last you all winter – AND I've just finished installing your Jacuzzi."

The Jello Master gave him a crushing look. "That, part of your training is! Learn respect and discipline, you must! Only then can you learn the secrets of the Source, Poo-poo!"

Puke stared at him in disgust. "And another thing – I'm fed up with you calling me Poo-poo." He shrugged out of his coveralls and stalked away. "So long, and thanks for nothin'!"

The Jello Master shook a gnarled fist. "Where do you think you going are? Finished resurfacing my patio, you have not!"

Puke swung himself into the cockpit of his stolen TOY fighter. "Forget it, small stuff. Find some other sucker!"

"Sorry, you will be!" screamed the infuriated Jello Master, dancing with rage.

However, as it turned out, Puke was not nearly as sorry as Yoggi. Standing carelessly behind the TOY fighter as Puke hit the ignition, the Jello Master was instantly fried in the rocket exhaust as Puke took off.

The shadowy figure of Old Dan hovered over the crisped remains of his former teacher.

"Someday, I'm gonna have to have a long talk with that boy," he mused.

The ghostly spirit of Yoggi popped into view just beside him. *"Ain't that the truth,"* observed the ex-Jello Master sourly.

Grabba the Gutt's spacebarge hovered above the asteroid home of the giant space slug. Between renewed fits of sneezing, the enraged creature stared up at the plank being extended from the side of the ship. It licked its lips with a tongue the length of an interstate freeway.

Finally dragged from their filthy prison cells to stand before the evil Gutt, Hans Zup and Choccibikki prepared to meet their fate with quiet dignity and pride.

"Hey, c'mon, Grabba, lighten up, will ya?" whined Hans. "Anyhow, it was all his fault." He pointed an accusing finger at Choccibikki.

"Guuuurrrroooaaaawwww," protested the outraged Cookie.

"You mugs think you've got problems?" Liar winced as the vile crime lord planted another slimy, slobbery kiss on her twitching cheek. "Will you get a load of these duds?" She gazed down in disgust at the dancing-girl costume Grabba had forced her to wear. "Lime green and peach – I ask you, who in the Galaxy could carry that off?"

"Ho . . . ho . . . ho," rumbled her tormentor. ***"Arrividerciroma! Forauldlangsyne! Sayonaraaloha!"***

"So long, suckers," translated Doe Raymefar, with an ironic little wave.

Far below, the terrible space slug slavered in anticipation as Grabba's henchthings mercilessly prodded the luckless Hans and Choccibikki toward their doom. They inched fearfully along the plank at whose end lay the long drop to certain death.

Just as Hans felt himself teetering on the very edge of the plank, he suddenly became aware of yells and screams behind him. Looking around in confusion, he saw Grabba's creatures fleeing for their lives as a TOY fighter, clearly out of control, hurtled toward the side of the spacebarge.

With a thunderous screech of tortured metal, the small ship embedded itself in the side of the barge. The unwieldy vessel tilted alarmingly. Hans's feet slid from under him. He twisted in midair, his desperately scrabbling fingers catching the very edge of the plank. As he hung there, his arms feeling as though they were being pulled from their sockets, Choccibikki plummeted past him and managed to grab hold of one of Hans's boots with a giant paw.

Seconds later, the dazed and disoriented figure of Puke Moonwalker scrambled out of the fighter and found himself surrounded by a host of vengeful guards led by Bobbi Sox. Puke raised his Power Sword above his head in the time-honored attack posture of the Jello Knight. "By the power of the Source!" he cried in a mighty voice. He stepped forward and whirled the energy blade in a dazzling arc before switching the weapon off and presenting it, hilt-first, to Bobbi Sox as a token of surrender. Then he threw himself on the floor, hands clasped behind his head.

Liar, meanwhile, had taken advantage of the distraction to snuggle closer to Grabba.

"Hey, big boy," she breathed into what she hoped was the Gutt's ear, "why don't you and me get to know each other a little better while the boys have their fun?"

Grabba gave her a loathsome leer. ***"Ho . . . ho . . . ho."***

"C'mon, why don't I get you a little snack before we get friendly?" Liar reached for a plate of exotic fruits. "How's about a nice, succulent hyperlychee?"

Grabba took the fruit between his blubbery lips and swallowed it whole. ***"Ho . . . ho . . . ho."***

"Now, how's about a yummy maximango?"

"Ho . . . ho . . . ho."

"And just to finish up, here's a big juicy pineapple." Liar produced a green metallic fruitlike object and shoved it into the monster's ravening maw.

Grabba swallowed. His eyes widened in shock. ***"Watchatryna pullya dumbroad?"*** he roared.

Doe Raymefar translated. "The Great Grabba says, 'Did that pineapple have a pin in it?'"

"Not anymore," replied Liar, diving for cover.

Grabba exploded.

The blast swept the decks clear of the Gutt's hirelings. Bobbi Sox was blown clear over the rail of the spacebarge and sent spinning helplessly into the waiting jaws of the space slug.

Liar raised her head and grimaced. "Oh boy! Hate to be the contract cleaner who gets this job."

Realizing that his foes were defenseless, Puke leaped to his feet. Recovering his Power Sword, he struck out around him like a maniac, cutting a swathe through Grabba's demoralized and disoriented crew.

"Hey, kid! Over here!" All his attempts to shake off the panic-stricken Cookie having failed, Hans gazed beseechingly at Puke for help.

Immediately breaking off from a frenzied attack on a fear-crazed creature fully half his size, Puke ran to the end of the plank and stamped on Hans's clutching fingers with his steel-tipped spaceboots.

"Hey! Cut that out!" Reluctantly, Puke desisted at Princess Liar's outraged order. With extreme unwillingness, he reached down to help first the trembling Hans, and then the petrified Cookie, onto the safety of the plank.

Shortly afterward, standing on the bridge of the *Millennium Bug*, Hans, Puke, Liar, Choccibikki, and the droids watched the last moments of the crippled barge as it sank into the space slug's waiting maw.

"I owe you one, kiddo," Hans whispered savagely in Puke's ear.

Liar turned. "Now boys," she said chidingly, "you aren't fighting over li'l ol' me, are you?"

Hans and Puke looked down at their feet. "No'm," they mumbled in unison.

"Good." Liar pointed to Sola Teedoe. "Let's get this little droid to the last GOODIES base. We've got some unfinished business with Dark Visor."

Towing the slightly bent TOY fighter, the *Millennium Bug* lurched away from the scene of battle.

At the same moment, far away on the control bridge of the Moon of Doom™, a helmeted figure watched a point of light begin to move against a giant star chart, away from an asteroid belt and toward the long-sought base of his enemies.

Dark Visor's rasping breath grew harsh with anticipation.

"**Hurrr'haaa, Hurrr'haaa, Hurrr'haaa!** Now I have them!"

CHAPTER TWELVE

Use the Source, Puke . . .

After what seemed like days, but was in fact weeks, the *Millennium Bug* and Puke's stolen TOY fighter reached the last remaining GOODIES base on the third moon of the planet Yonkers. As the ships touched down, they were surrounded by cheering GOODIES fighters. Liar descended from the *Bug* and was greeted by Admiral Fishface, commander of the GOODIES forces.

"Welcome, Your Highness. Glad you could make it."

"Thanks, Fishface."

The rest of the group descended from the two ships

to deafening applause. Choccibikki was immediately surrounded by dozens of small furry creatures that looked like miniature Cookies.

Sola Teedoe and Doe Raymefar moved among the chuckling creatures. "What sweet and lovely creatures they are . . . The sickly little furballs should be skinned and made into coats," snarled Doe Raymefar.

"They're Chocci's cousins," Hans explained to Liar. "They're called Awacs. They have an incredible ability to sense danger before it happens. Amazing little guys."

Suddenly all the Awacs' heads turned skyward. As one they stood stock-still. Their eyes grew wide, and their little hairy noses began to twitch. "Bye-bye!" they squeaked. Then they shot off as quickly as their legs could carry them.

Within seconds the base was Awac-less.

"Why have they run away?" queried Liar

"Admiral Fishface, sir." A GOODIE Rebel held out a piece of data paper. "This has just come through on the radar scan."

The Admiral took the paper and stared at it. "The Moon of Doom™ is approaching!"

Liar flinched. "The Moon of Doom™? How did Visor know we were here?"

Hans shook his head, "I don't know, fudge cake, but I do know we're in deep doo-doo!"

"Wwaaaarrrrrrrrr!" agreed Choccibikki, hurriedly climbing into a flak jacket, a steel helmet, and a sixty-foot-deep concrete bunker.

A few hours later, the ranks of GOODIES spacefighters crowded into the mission briefing room. They had gathered from all over the known Universe. They had one common cause: to overthrow the BADDIES and restore peace, harmony, and love to the Universe.

"Hippie good-for-nothings," snarled Doe Raymefar as he viewed the assembled ranks.

Choccibikki and Hans sat next to Puke at the back of the room. The droids were at the front, sitting next to the Princess and Admiral Fishface.

Standing alongside this group was a tall humanoid from the planet Gungho. He had a large red mustache and was pointing at a data screen.

"Thanks for coming, chaps. You all know why we're here, so we'll take all the 'saving the Universe and restoring harmony and peace' bit as read. Now, a bit of bad news, I'm afraid. The Moon of Doom™ will be arriving in Yonkers' orbit in the next few hours. It is, without question, the most destructive weapon ever created in the Universe. It has the capability of blasting us all into tiny bits. Not only that, it is commanded by the most evil being ever known, who will order our destruction without even batting an eyelid. Any problems so far?"

There was a collective gulp from the GOODIES.

The Gunghonian smiled a winning smile. "However, it's not as bad as it sounds!"

He motioned toward Sola Teedoe. "Thanks to our brave little friend here, we have managed to obtain top-secret plans of the Moon of Doom™."

"*Hih . . . hih . . . hih . . . hih . . .* Dweep." The little droid acknowledged the plaudits.

"Creep," muttered Doe Raymefar.

"Thanks to these plans, we know where to find the Moon of Doom's™ Achilles' heel."

He flashed up a diagram of the Moon of Doom™ and pointed to a tiny dot on its side. "This is a fuel discharge pipe. By a staggering coincidence, it leads to the main nuclear reactor. You may say that this is a major design fault, I say it is a piece of good fortune. Our experts reckon that if we manage to hit this fuel pipe with a couple of photon torpedoes, there will be a nuclear reaction, and the whole darn Moon thing will blow up like a puffball in a strong wind!"

The GOODIES cheered.

"Now, our experts have made some computer predictions and say that the mission will be easily achieved by using two hundred fifty-six spacefighters in a carefully coordinated collective attack." The Gunghonian paused. His mustache began to twitch. "However, we've got a teeny-weeny problem. We seem to have a small shortfall in this area. A shortfall of some two hundred fifty-five fighters. To be blunt, we have only *one* serviceable ship – the one that young Puke Moonwalker stole from the BADDIES."

"What about the *Bug*?" called out Puke. Hans gave him a filthy look.

"I did say a *serviceable* ship."

Hans scowled.

"So, in a nutshell, we've got one spacefighter – so we need one pilot. All that idiot . . ." He coughed. "I mean, all that *brave pilot* needs to do is fly up to the Moon of Doom™, avoid the whole BADDIES fleet on the way, dodge all the lasers, phasers, cannons, and so forth, and send a couple of torpedoes down the fuel pipe that measures no more than a few centimeters across, blow the whole darn thing to oblivion, and then return home for lavish hurrahs and congratulations."

The Gunghonian looked around the room. "So who'd like to volunteer?"

There was a deathly silence.

Puke turned to Hans and whispered under his breath, "You'd have to be absolutely crazy to volunteer. It's a suicide mission."

Hans nodded slowly as he plucked a badge from his tunic. "You don't say," he hissed before jamming the badge's pin into Puke's backside.

"Oewwwarrggghhh!" Puke shot up from his seat.

"A volunteer!" cried Admiral Fishface.

"Er, not really – I just . . ." But before Puke could say anything else, he was stopped by Liar, who had run to the back of the hall and begun kissing him.

"I hate you, Puke," said Liar.

"Likewise," hissed Hans.

Amidst crowds of cheering GOODIES, Puke headed toward the fighter, with Liar draped on his arm. As he left the room, Puke glanced over at Hans, who was sitting at the back of the hall, biting his lip so hard it was bleeding.

"Don't come back," smiled Liar.

Puke sped toward the Moon's defenses, struggling with the controls of the TOY fighter, which seemed to have a mind of its own. Puke's hand slipped on the joystick, causing his fighter to spin so wildly out of control that three chasing BADDIES fighters crashed into each other in surprise.

Leaving a trail of confused BADDIES pilots in his wake after another wild sideslip, Puke found himself nearing the huge weapon of destruction that was the Moon of Doom™. Space around his ship was suddenly clear. Puke felt elated. The fighters had given up! He was going to make it!

Then a fusillade of electrobolts, lasers, and photon cannons began to shoot from the surface of the Moon of Doom™ in a deadly hail of destruction.

Puke closed his eyes and waited for his inevitable end.

In that moment of despair, he heard a comforting voice.

"Use the horse, Puke lad. Use the horse."

Puke looked around "What horse, Dan?" he cried.

"Sorry lad, it must be a bad line. Don't use a horse, that would be silly. Ye must use the Source, lad. Give yourself over to the Source. Clear your mind, think of nothing, breathe deeply, relax . . . relax . . . relax . . ."

"Zzzzzzzzzzzzzzzzzzzzzzz."

"Wake up, Puke!"

Puke jolted out of the depths of sleep. He was heading straight for an oncoming BADDIES fighter! Its pilot banked his fighter hard to avoid Puke. It spun away, hit the side of the Moon of Doom™, and exploded in a huge orange fireball.

"Way to go, Puke lad . . ."

Then another voice penetrated Puke's mind.

"Poo-poo. Here am I, Yoggi. Thought I be of help might, as mess complete Old Dan is making."

"I am not, Yoggi lad. Leave this to me, Old Dan can handle it."

"Think you can, I don't . . ."

"Will you two stop arguing!" screamed Puke. "I need some help here!"

Puke pushed the fighter down into the Moon of Doom's™ metal canyons.

Cannons roared to the right of him, cannons roared to the left of him, into the canyon of death flew Puke Moonwalker.

"Left a bit, Puke lad."

"No, right."

"Straight ahead."

"To the left, not straight be your course."

"Left."

"Right."

"Left."

The stolen fighter was careering all over the canyon. The pursuing BADDIES TOY fighters tried in vain to second-guess which way Puke's ship would veer. They overshot and undershot, with the upshot that they went crashing into the unforgiving metal walls.

From deep within Puke's mind another voice seemed to emerge. A woman's voice. Liar's voice. "I'm with you, Puke. Use the Source."

A deep calm overtook Puke's mind. He could see everything before him. He knew what he had to do. He was no longer in control of flying his fighter. It was being guided by the Source.

The opening to the fuel pipe was fast approaching. He flicked the switch down on the missile launch system. *Steady, steady*, he told himself.

"This is for you, Dad," he whispered.

He hit the missile button

"Fwoooshhhhhh." The two photon torpedoes flashed through the vacuum. Moments later, they disappeared into the fuel discharge pipe.

Puke pulled back hard on the controls, and his fighter zoomed up nearly vertically into the blackness of space and away from the Moon of Doom™.

"Yeeehhhaaaaaahhh!" screamed Puke. He waited for the huge explosion . . .

And waited . . .

And waited . . .

An urgent voice crackled over Puke's radio. It was Admiral Fishface. As he listened, Puke began to feel his stomach tighten.

"What do you mean, the wrong pipe?" he asked.

The radio crackled again.

"Oh, you meant the *red* pipe over *there*? I'm sorry, I thought you meant the *blue* one over *here* . . ."

The Moon of Doom™ was still intact.

CHAPTER THIRTEEN

My Dad's a Dread Lord!

An air of gloom had settled over the GOODIES base. In a few short hours, the Moon of Doom™ would arrive and the GOODIES would be wiped off the face of the Galaxy.

Hans, Liar, Chocci, and the Droids sat slumped beside an anemic-looking campfire. Hans poked fretfully at the ashes.

"What a bummer," he muttered.

Nobody looked up as Puke slouched into the clearing.

"Er . . . guys . . ." Puke began. He cleared his throat

and started again. "I guess you guys are thinking this is all my fault."

Nobody spoke.

"So I was thinking I'd go and fly out to the Moon of Doom™ and give myself up." Puke swallowed. "Maybc I can talk Dark Visor into leaving the rest of you alone."

Hans shrugged and stoked the fire. "Good idea," he said flatly.

Princess Liar nodded. "I'll go with that."

"Hrrroaaawwwrrr!" agreed the Cookie.

"My mind's made up," said Puke. "Don't try and stop me!"

"We weren't going to."

"Oh. Right." Bowed with the burden of his guilt, Puke turned and shambled away. He hadn't gone far when there was a clatter behind him. Puke sighed with relief.

"Oh, okay, you talked me out of it . . ."

"It's only me, sir – ya useless dumb cluck – sorry . . ." Doe Raymefar slapped the side of his head. "I thought I'd come with you – if you don't mind."

"You?" Puke stared at the droid. Then his lip trembled. His eyes brimmed with tears as he patted the droid on the shoulder. "Thank you, my faithful old friend. Let's go."

Head hanging low with misery, Puke trudged on toward his stolen fighter. Behind him, Doe Raymefar's eyes glowed in the dark.

"Lord Visor!" The orderly snapped off a salute. "We have captured a GOODIES spy, and his droid. They were brought in by one of our patrol ships a few moments ago."

Visor clenched his fists. "Bring them to me!"

He turned to a figure sitting in the shadows on the opposite side of the control bridge. A figure wearing simple robes and a hood that hid his face almost entirely from view. A figure that exuded an almost overpowering sense of menace.

Dark Visor bowed low before his master, Emperor Palpitate, Master of the BADDIES and Supreme Ruler of the Whole Galaxy. "Moonwalker is here, my Master. Now the Rebels will be utterly crushed. Together, we will destroy the last of the Jello Knights."

"Yessiree," cackled an ancient voice. "That's what we'll do, yessiree bob. Then we can find out who's been hiding my teeth all these years. Didja bring the chicken noodle soup, Mother? I'm ninety-seven, you know!"

Dark Visor groaned. Master of the Downside or not, the Emperor was clearly well past his sell-by date. He would have to go.

Guards brought in Puke and Doe Raymefar. At Visor's imperious gesture, they turned and left.

"Oh, dear." The droid backed up against a wall and stood there, unmoving.

"So, Moonwalker, at last you have seen the futility

of resistance," hissed the Dread Lord.

"You betcha!" cackled the Emperor. "Kids today, who can figure 'em? There's too much starch in these shorts! Somebody took the paper! I don't like oatmeal!"

"So, what am I to do with you . . ." Visor paused, and then went on, "my son?"

Puke gazed at him in shock. "You cannot be serious!" He shook his head. "You can't be my father! My father is dead. Old Dan told me. He said you betrayed my father!"

"Hey," snapped Visor, "are you going to believe that old four-flusher, or are you going to believe me? So I got hooked on the Downside, no problem, I can give it up any time I like . . ." The raging Dread Lord pulled himself together. "That is why I brought you here, Puke. The Source is strong in you – and in your sister."

"I don't have a sister!" Puke stared at Visor. A horrible thought struck him. "You don't mean . . . that freckly girl on Toonilooni with the overbite and knock-knees who keeps asking me to . . .?"

"No, you idiot!" thundered Visor. "I mean Princess Liar! Liar is your sister!"

"Oh no!" Puke gave a moan of despair and wiped his mouth on the back of his hand. "Perfect!"

"So tell me, my son . . ." Visor leaned forward. "Why have you come here?"

Glancing nervously at the Emperor, Puke pulled himself together, and spoke. "Lord Visor, my Lord Emperor, you are both powerful and great. Now is the time to show that you are wise as well."

The old man in the robes began to make a gagging sound. Puke pressed on. "No tyranny has ever lasted. No government that has raised itself to power without the will of the people has ever stood the test of time."

The noise from the figure became a desperate gargling. "With great power comes great responsibility. You have the power to destroy the GOODIES . . . or embrace them."

The gargling became a despairing rattle. Puke turned from Visor to the Emperor in a desperate appeal. "My lords, you have the chance to show true greatness. You can plunge the Galaxy into a dark age of war and strife, or . . ." Puke paused for effect. "You can begin a new era of hope, peace, and universal brotherhood! Therefore, I ask you to spare the GOODIES – not because you cannot destroy them . . . but because you can." Puke bowed his head.

There was a thump as the Emperor's head fell against the arm of his chair.

Dark Visor checked for a pulse and shook his head. "I'm afraid you bored him to death," he said reproachfully. "He was very old."

Visor straightened up. "So, the Emperor is dead." He reached for the Power Sword at his belt and ignited it. Raising it aloft, he said softly, "And now it's your turn."

Puke gazed at the glittering blade in horror. "But, Father . . . wait!" he squeaked. "You don't have to kill me – don't you see?" Puke edged away from the sword. His father followed his every movement. "Suppose I was to come over to the Downside of the Source . . . like you . . . now that the Emperor's gone, we could rule the Galaxy together, father and son . . . whaddya say?"

The deadly blade never wavered. Visor's voice was harsh. "Do you think I've worked myself to death all these years to get where I am, just to let some little whippersnapper stab me in the back first chance he gets? Oh no, son, I'm afraid this is where you get yours. No more Mr. Nice Guy!"

"VERZANG!"

"VERZENG!"

"VERZING!"

"VERZONG!"

"VERZUNG!"

"VERZAEIOUNG!"

Puke stared at thc Dread Lord. "Are you just going to stand there making silly noises all night?"

With a roar of rage, Dark Visor launched into the attack.

Ducking under a table, Puke scrabbled desperately for his own Power Sword. Igniting it, he desperately warded off Visor's hammer blows.

The battle had begun.

Back and forth across the control room, the two Jello Knights, father and son, fought. Blades leaped and clashed in a fury of blinding light. Equipment shattered by wayward sword strokes shot plumes of sparks across the room, adding to the confusion. In a breathtaking display of agility, Puke leaped a full six inches off the ground and brought his Power Sword down on Visor's gloved fist. The blade sliced through skin and bone, sending Visor's severed hand, and the Power Sword it held, slithering into a dark corner.

Breathing like a pair of ruptured bellows, Visor backed away from Puke's sword.

Puke raised his weapon for the fatal blow. "So long, Pops!"

From behind Puke came a voice that stopped him in his tracks.

"I have a laser pistol in my hand. It is pointing straight at the back of your head. Drop . . . your . . . sword!"

CHAPTER FOURTEEN

The Moon of Doom™ Goes Kaboom!

Puke turned. The figure pointing a laser pistol unwaveringly at his head was . . .

"Doe Raymefar!"

"Well it ain't Sola Teedoe, knucklehead!" Doe Raymefar slowly moved toward Puke, motioning him to drop his sword.

"What are you doing?" asked Puke, his mind in a whirl.

Taking advantage of this surprising turn of events, Visor began to sidle over toward his Power Sword.

"Don't move, Visor!" Puke shouted. "Or else . . ."

A blast from Doe Raymefar's pistol shot over Puke's head, causing him to drop his own weapon.

"Don't you hurt my daddy!" the droid cried.

"Your daddy?" gasped Puke, "But Visor's my daddy!"

"Yes, but he was *my* daddy first." The deranged droid gazed adoringly at Visor. "Tell him, Daddy."

Puke looked at Doe Raymefar and Visor in astonishment.

"Is this true?"

"**Hurrr'haaa, Hurrrr' haaa**," rasped the Dread Lord.

"I'll take that as a yes."

Doe Raymefar's grip on the pistol's trigger tightened. The droid moved toward Puke.

Puke stood defiantly before his father and half(ish) brother. He stuck out his chin and gathered himself up. "If you think I'm going to go down on my knees and beg for my life like some yellow, spineless spacewimp . . . you're absolutely right! Have merceeeey!"

He dropped his sword, threw himself to the ground, and began beating the floor with his fists.

The droid moved in for the kill. Puke looked up into the cold, dark stare of his father.

"At least give me an explanation. I'm your son, too."

Doe Raymefar shot Puke a jealous look.

Visor considered the request. He motioned to Doe Raymefar. "Wait."

"But he's just stalling, Daddy."

"All in good time, son." The Dread Lord lit a corncob

pipe and sat back in his command chair, rocking gently. "Once, I was a callow youth, like you are now. Long before I became Dark Visor, I went by the name of Animosity Moonwalker. I always enjoyed tinkering with machines. I scrounged all kinds of metal junk from scrap yards and spaceship wrecks – a diode here, a resistor there – and gradually, piece by piece, part by part, I built a droid of my very own."

Doe Raymefar's voice choked with emotion. "That's my daddy who did that."

"I rediscovered him at Riks Bar on Toonilooni, and sent him to be my spy on the *Millennium Bug*. He helped me locate the secret GOODIES base."

Puke gazed at the droid with hatred. "You traitor!"

Visor knocked his pipe out and stood up. "And now he will help me destroy you and your Rebel friends – and then he and I shall rule the Galaxy, together!"

Overcome with emotion, Doe Raymefar flung himself into Visor's arms. "I love you, Daddy!"

Puke saw his chance and leaped for his sword.

VERZZZANG!

Visor saw the danger too late. He barely managed to block Puke's furious assault. Doe Raymefar began blasting away with his laser pistol. By some miracle of coincidence and narrative improbability, Puke's wildly erratic swordplay blocked every one of Dark Visor's lunges and every bolt of laser energy fired at him by the maddened droid.

Through the corridors of the Moon of Doom™ the

battle raged. Father and metal son versus fleshy son. The air hummed and lit up with rainbow-colored streams of laser bolts and flashing arcs from Power Swords.

As Puke staggered backward under the force of the combined attack, he felt a chill blast of air on his back. He glanced around and gasped. He was standing on the edge of the Abyss of Oblivion.

Visor towered above him. “There is no escaping, Puke,” he rasped. “It is your destiny to die, as it is my destiny to rule.” With a powerful thrust, Visor brought his sword smashing down.

VERZANGGGGGGGGGGGGGGG!

Sword met sword.

Puke cried out in despair as his weapon was wrenched from his grip. He stared helplessly as the sword went spinning into the void of the Abyss.

“And now the end is near . . .” Visor moved in for the kill. Doe Raymefar stood behind him and glowed with pride.

Summoning all the power of the Source, Puke leaped high into the air. His body flicked into a series of complicated spins and twists as he flew over the heads of Visor and Doe Raymefar.

With a perfectly executed back flip, Puke bounced off the far metal wall, hurtled back, and launched a flying drop kick at his startled foes.

As one, Visor and Doe Raymefar ducked.

With a deafening scream, Puke plunged into the Abyss.

The *Millennium Bug*, rigged for silent running, slid sneakily out of the atmosphere of the GOODIES' moon.

Hans held the throttle levers shoved down as far as they would go. If the Moon of Doom™ caught them before they were ready to make the jump to hyperspace . . .

Dratted ship repair yard! They'd promised to finish repairing the *Bug* on Tuesday!

Princess Liar bit her lip. "I don't know why I let you talk me into this. It's against all my principles to run away."

"We're not running away," Hans told her. "We're effecting a strategic withdrawal to a previously prepared position."

"What position?"

"A position very far away from this base."

Liar continued to fret. "I hate sneaking away like this, knowing that all my friends down there are going to die when the Moon of Doom™ gets here."

Hans stared at her. "Listen, sweetie pie, I know one thing that's a whole lot worse than knowing your friends are going to die."

"And what might that be?"

"Knowing that you're going to die with them."

"Wrrrooooaaaawwwrrrrrr!" Choccibikki pointed a trembling furry finger toward the cockpit window, and started writing his will.

Hans gazed out and saw the Moon of Doom™ emerging from the shadow of Yonkers. "Here it comes!" he grated.

Liar gripped the back of the pilot's chair. "We'll never get away!" she gasped.

Hans gave a fierce grin. "Don't worry, doll. I had the tech boys back at the base fix the old *Bug* up good. They installed a new computer. We're outside the gravity well now – time to make the jump to hyperspace!" He flicked a series of switches. "Computer, take us into hyperspace."

"I'm sorry, Dave . . . I mean Hans." The new computer had a soft, mellow, apologetic voice. "I'm afraid I can't do that right now."

Hans groaned and held his head in his hands.

"That's it, then," said Liar resignedly. "We are definitely going to die."

"Owwoooaaaarrrrwwwllllll," agreed Choccibikki, tying a blindfold over his eyes and lighting a cigarette.

"Uselessbozohanszup . . . beep . . . *Hih . . . hih . . . hih . . . hih . . .*" added Sola Teedoe.

The Moon of Doom™ grew larger, until it filled the cockpit windows.
Enormous laser crystals began to glow, and the terrible battle station prepared to unleash its devastating power against the GOODIES base and the helpless *Bug*.

Hans, Liar, Choccibikki, and Sola Teedoe waited for the end.

On the bridge of the Moon of Doom™, Doe Raymefar put his arms around Dark Visor's body. He wrapped himself up in the Dread Lord's cloak. Oily tears sprang from his eyes. "Daddy!"

"Son." Visor ruffled the droid's metal head.

"Don't ever leave me again," whined Doe Raymefar.

"Don't worry, son, I won't. It's going to be me and you now."

Father and son stood gazing out at the great expanse of space. Stars twinkled in the majesty of the firmament. Moons and otherworlds beckoned. Visor pointed his stump at the vastness. "One day, son, all this will be yours."

Hisssssssss.

"What was that?" Visor spun around.

The hissing noise grew louder.

"It's a hissing noise, Daddy."

"I know that!"

A terrible realization began to creep slowly into the Dread Lord's mind. "Son, when you were firing that pistol like you were Billy the Droid, did you shoot anywhere near the life-support system?

"Possibly."

The realization was beginning to travel at the speed of light.

"And when you were 'possibly' firing near the life-support system, did you by any chance notice if any shots hit the *Atmosphere Dump Control Panel*?"

Doe Raymefar thought for a second. "As a matter of fact, I think they did," he nodded. "What does an *Atmosphere Dump* do?"

"It blows all the air out of the station, you stupid boy."

"DOHHHHHHHHHHH!"

Visor and Doe Raymefar were picked up and whirled around like snowflakes as air shot from the Moon of Doom™. The giant space station began to deflate like a pricked balloon.

It hit a distant star and exploded in a shimmering fireball.

PHAAAAAAAAAAAAAAAAAAAAAAAAAAAAAAAAAAAAAAAAAAAAAAARRRRRRRRRRRRRRRRRRRRRRRRRRRPPPPPPPPPPPPPPPPPPPPPP

BANG!

Hurled from the Moon of Doom™ by the rush of escaping air, Puke shot out into space like a champagne cork.

He fell through the cold vacuum of space – a fall that would last for a thousand eons, unless he happened to hit something first. But the chances of that, thought Puke as he prepared for inevitable death, were infinitesimal.

At that moment, he hit something very hard with a resounding THUD.

Hans gazed in astonishment at the figure of Puke spread-eagled against the cockpit window. He shook his head. "You have got to be kiddin' me."

"Quick!" Liar shook his arm. "He can't survive in space. Get him inside the ship or he'll die horribly in a matter of seconds."

Hans gave her a sideways look. "This is a problem?"

"Do it!"

With a sigh, Hans turned to Sola Teedoe. "Go out there and bring the washout in."

Sola Teedoe backed off. "*Innapigseyebub . . . Hih . . . hih . . . hih . . . hih . . .*"

Hans gave the little droid an ingratiating leer. "You'll get a medal."

Sola Teedoe trembled with excitement. "*Merral! Merral! Gimmegimmegimme! Beep! Yehyehyehyehyehyeh . . . Hih . . . hih . . . hih . . . hih . . .*"

Seconds later, Sola Teedoe had hauled Puke's unresisting body through the airlock to safety.

The whole Galaxy celebrated the downfall of the evil BADDIES.

On the capital world of Corusline, a multitude of cheering citizens from every planet in the new Commonwealth of Independent Worlds gathered to greet their heroes – the Zero-Gravity Basketball Team that had just beaten Andromeda 156 to 40.

Meanwhile, in the bar of a cheap spaceport hotel, Puke, Hans, Chocci, and Liar prepared to go their separate ways.

Liar squeezed Puke's arm. "Too bad you had to pawn the droids."

Puke sighed. "No choice when that bill came through from the Defense Department." He pulled out a crumpled bill and read: "Item: malicious damage to Ultimate Secret Weapon: 39,000,000,000,000,000,000,000,000,000,000 Galactibucks. Failure to submit payment within 31 days may do lasting damage to your credit rating."

Liar turned to Hans. "And you had to sell the *Bug*, too."

Hans shrugged. "Only way I could pay the damages when the survivors of Grabba's spacebarge sued me for causing them distress and mental suffering." The *Bug*'s ex-captain stood and faced the Princess. "And now it's time, angel-face."

"Time?" Liar was mystified. "What time?"

"Time to choose." Hans stuck his chin out and stuck his thumbs in his belt. "Is it gonna be Puke – or me?"

"Oh, hey, Liar!" Puke snapped his fingers. "Before you say anything, I think I just ought to mention that you're my sister. Sorry, meant to tell you, completely slipped my mind."

Liar stared at him. "Your *sister?*"

"Yup."

As Puke told her the story, Liar pawed frantically at her mouth. "But I *kissed* you! Oh, yuck! Mega-maxi gross-out! I'm going to wash my mouth out with soap. And disinfectant. And bleach. I'm going to sandpaper my lips off! Yeeeuuurrrggh!"

"Hey!" Puke was peeved. "Don't get so agitated."

"And you didn't even tell me?"

"I forgot, okay?"

"I hate you! You're just a stupid little kid! You give me a pain!"

"Well, you give me a pain, too!

"Yaah!"

"Yaah yourself!"

Hans watched the developing brother-and-sister relationship with a broad grin on his face. "Well, guess that just leaves me, cutie pie."

Liar gave him a withering look. "Think again, slimeball." She flung her arms around the Cookie. "Did you get the tickets, Chocci-poos?"

Hans and Puke stared at her in disbelief. *"Chocci-poos?"*

Liar winked at them. "Hey, he'll save me a fortune in fur coats."

"Rooaarrrrwwwwl," agreed the Cookie.

She blew them a kiss. "Ciao, boys. It's been a blast."

And then she was gone.

Epilogue

Many months later, two beat-up-looking spacers sat in Riks Bar on the sand-swept planet of Toonilooni. The table in front of them was littered with empty glasses and bottles.

Hans gazed blearily at the grubby cards in his hand. His eyes narrowed as he gazed across at Puke, who met his stare with an expressionless face.

Hans shrugged and slid several of his dwindling pile of chips to the much larger pile in the center of the table.

Speaking very slowly and clearly, he said, "Have you got Mrs. Baaglrgflar, the Eight-Eyed Methane Delivery Man's Wife?"

Puke shook his head. "Nope."

With a despairing sigh, Hans shoved the whole pile of chips over to Puke's side of the table. Puke ate them.

"You know, buddy," said Hans, "all those months we spent hitchin' our way back to this dustball, I got to thinkin'. You know what?"

"What?"

"We don't never got to let a dame stand between us again. Right?"

Puke slammed his fist on the table. "Right!"

Hans nodded wisely. "I mean, dames is poison. Right?"

"Right!" Puke pointed unsteadily at Hans. "You're my best buddy, you know that?"

"Awww . . ."

"So I'm gonna tell you what I never told nobody before. When I got back here, my aunt Dorify gave me my dad's old diary."

"Your dad?"

"Dark Visor, remember?"

Hans waved a hand vaguely. "Right, right."

"Only this was before he was Dark Visor, when he was just a kid, here on Toonilooni." Puke pulled a battered book out of his pocket, and began to read.

Through the long afternoon, scattered fragments of Puke's story floated through the open windows of the bar to fade into silence in the stifling desert air.

" . . . . . . blockade . . . . . . Oblah-Dee Oblah-Dan . . . . . . Quid Pro Quo, the Jello Master . . . . . . Princess of the Nanki-poo . . . . . . Rodraces . . . . . . Ha-ha Bigjoke . . . . Panting Menace . . . . . . Dark Mole . . . . . . Yoggi . . . . . ."

Finally, Puke shut the book with a snap. "And they all lived happily for a disappointingly short period of time," he said dreamily.

Hans, looking suddenly alert, was fumbling in his pocket for his hyperphone. "You told anybody about this book yet?"

Puke shook his head.

"Listen, kid." Hans began furiously punching numbers on the phone's keypad. "I'm gonna call a guy I know –

he's in the movies. That story you got there . . ." He held the phone to his ear. " . . . sounds like it could make a great prequel . . ."

THE MIDDLE